THUMBS UP!

THUMBS UP!

By

RUTHERFORD G. MONTGOMERY

Illustrated by

E. FRANKLIN WITTMACK

DAVID McKAY COMPANY
WASHINGTON SQUARE · PHILADELPHIA

CONTENTS

THUMBS
UP!

CHAPTER 1 LEATHERNECKS

THE CIRCLE of the horizon was the rim of a vast, blue bowl of water and upon this rim rested an even vaster blue bowl of sky. Dawn was breaking over the Pacific island of Paris. It came like a light being switched on in a dark room, a red glow which radiated upward and lighted the dark surface of the ocean.

Three men sat on a sand dune and looked toward the east. Paris Island was just a speck in that vast universe. Lying flat and round like a pancake, with breakers sliding in upon its sandy beach and then sliding out again, it looked no different than a thousand other specks in the vast Pacific. The only visible landmarks on the island were two low buildings, a hangar and a row of barracks. Back of the barracks rose a clump of struggling palm trees.

"I joined the marines for action," Lieutenant Michael O'Toole growled as he dug his heels into the sand. "What do I get?"

"A nice restful spot far out in the Pacific where you can commune with your soul," Lieutenant Marty Rivers answered with a grin. Rivers was tall and broad shouldered. In swallowing him up, Paris Island had deprived sports photographers of a very popular subject, an All-American halfback who had made headlines in pro football after graduation.

The third member of the trio said nothing. Captain Mel Edwards had been a marine since he was eighteen. Now, at twenty-five, he was captain in charge of Marine Aircraft, Group Eleven 13 at Outpost Ten. His equipment consisted of six Grumman Wildcats and a Vought-Sikorsky amphibian used for utility transport. Captain Edwards had come up from the ranks.

He had learned all that there is to know about the duties of a marine.

"If we'd joined up with the R.A.F., we'd be knocking Messerschmitts out of the sky right now," O'Toole grumbled. His thatch of red hair bristled and his huge Adam's apple rolled up and down his long neck. O'Toole had been a Texas cotton-duster, commonly known as a boll weevil. Marine Corps flying irked him after his experiences in dusting pecan groves— where a pilot, an hour before dawn, flew between tree rows with his landing wheels a few feet off the ground.

"You forget the Japs," Edwards said shortly.

"Japs!" O'Toole snorted. "We're twelve hundred miles from Manila and twice that far from any Jap base. Those yellow pygmies don't interest O'Toole at all."

"Think of the ultra-violet rays we get all day long, and the graceful sea gulls wheeling overhead, and the fine swimming," Marty Rivers said with a broad grin.

O'Toole got to his feet. He stood looking up

the beach toward the three Grumman Wildcats
that had been rolled out ready for the dawn patrol. The entire force of six ground men was
working with the planes. Long flames gutted
back from lazing exhausts and sand swirled away
in the blast from idling propellers. O'Toole
grinned just a little, his big mouth relaxing
loosely. Anyway those Wildcats were something
to play with, not like the slow and wobbly crates
a boll weevil had to put up with.

Captain Edwards got to his feet. He stared
out across the water, his mouth pulled into a grim
line. If his years of pushing into trouble spots
had taught him anything, that thing was eternal
vigilance. Marty Rivers rolled over and looked
up at him. He could never take marine life the
grim way. After all, this was peacetime patrol
—routine flights every day. Edwards was a
slave-driver. He never let up at all. It seemed
he felt he had the whole Pacific to patrol. Marty
yawned and got to his feet.

"We're off in half an hour," Edwards warned.

Marty looked up toward the hangars and

smiled. They had three replacement Wildcats and the Vought-Sikorsky. Some squadron! He dropped in beside Edwards and they started toward the hangar. O'Toole followed them. He was looking up at the palm grove, still grinning. The amphibian was hidden up there, just as though this were wartime. Hard-Face Edwards certainly was a suspicious man.

"She'll be collectin' barnacles in that damp jungle," he said, jerking his head toward the Vought-Sikorsky.

"She's safe," snapped Edwards.

Beyond the hangar the outpost squad of marines, under command of Major Delaney, had fallen in for morning drill. The major would put them through a workout consisting of a run around the island and gunnery practice. Sadly O'Toole shook his head. The marines sure took life seriously, lived it the hard way. After dawn patrol Edwards would swim his men around the island. O'Toole had never made up his mind which was worse, running around the atoll or swimming around it.

"Wait!" Captain Edwards barked.

The three fliers halted. Without much interest Marty and O'Toole gazed out to sea. Edwards was tense, scowling, his ears tuned to the pre-dawn sounds. After listening a full minute Marty heard motors. O'Toole fidgeted impatiently but calmed down when he caught the faint rumble.

"Planes," Marty said. "Must be another transport bringing some brass hats for an inspection."

"Looks like as many inspections as we've had, they'd finally make a real base out of this," O'Toole growled.

"No flight is scheduled," Edwards snapped. "We have had no radio reports of any flights."

Marty listened more intently. There was an unfamiliar pulsation in the rumble of the oncoming motors, and now there was no mistaking the fact that this was not one plane but a squadron.

"Get into your togs and take off!" Edwards barked.

O'Toole's slouching manner left him as he leaped forward with Marty beside him. They rushed into the little shack beside the hangar, which served as a briefing room. Edwards waited, standing on the beach, sweeping the sky with his binoculars.

"Anyway, we get to go sky riding a bit ahead of schedule," O'Toole muttered to himself as he clambered into his outfit.

Marty Rivers said nothing. He had a queer feeling along his spine, a feeling very close to a shiver.

"Those aren't U.S. Navy or Army planes," he said shortly.

"Bunk," O'Toole grunted. "They couldn't be anything else. You're a sucker for the stuff Edwards has been feedin' us. He's about made a marine out of you."

Waddling out of the shack with their parachutes rapping them across the legs, they saw Edwards diving for his Wildcat.

"He's going to beat us to it," Marty muttered.

"Look at the boys down there!" O'Toole shouted.

The marines under Major Delaney were rushing toward the shore batteries and the anti-aircraft guns, concealed back from the shore. The major was shouting so loud they could hear his orders.

Marty Rivers dived for his Wildcat. He was seeing plenty now. The black hulk of five battle-wagons loomed off the shore, suddenly revealed as the sun lifted the dark curtain of night from the ocean.

"I see the sign of the Rising Sun!" O'Toole shouted gleefully.

Marty clamped his lips tight. He was looking up into the sky where two wedges of twin-motored bombers were sloping down and peeling off in a businesslike manner. If this were a friendly call, it was being executed in a deadly manner.

There was no time for a decent take-off. Marty depressed one wheel brake, rammed the throttle knob up, and snapped the Wildcat hard around and lurched away. The Wildcat hoiked her tail with a blast of prop pressure and cantered off across the sand.

Edwards had a start, but Marty raged over his hatch cover and laid over sharply, so close to the ground his port wing sprayed sand and his prop ripped a great cloud of it into the air, blotting out completely O'Toole's plane.

"Steady, Patrol Flight, steady." Edwards' growl came in like the grating of sand on a board. "Up to three thousand. They have fighter support."

As he went up Marty saw under his wings a burst of flame and a great eruption of sand. From the sand rose pieces of their hangar and parts from the three Wildcats parked near the building.

"Looks like some fun," O'Toole's voice drawled.

Marty started to answer but his mouth was too dry to make a sound. He was zooming upward and over. As he came around he saw silver wings and bodies. The twin-motored killers were rising off their targets gracefully, in perfect formation.

"Attack the bombers!" Edwards rasped.

At that moment O'Toole shot over his hatch cover, roaring toward the three bombers. Marty laid over and dived at the nearest killer. As he went over he saw high above a dozen planes coming down the chute at a roaring pace. He guessed but wasn't sure that they were Kariganes. All he was sure of was that they had the key position for the kill.

O'Toole appeared not to have noticed the fighters. He had come up under one of the bombers and his Brownings were ripping death into the dural surface of the killer. Marty saw a wing flutter, then fold back. An instant later the bomber rolled over and dived. At the same instant the tail of a bomber showed in Marty's windscreen and he pressed his gun button. His wing guns flamed and the tail vanished from his vision.

Coming out of his dive close to the sandy beach, he saw that he had sent the bomber crashing over on her side. He also saw that Major Delaney's boys were hammering away with their three-inch and five-inch guns and that the battlewagons were answering with roaring broadsides.

"This must be war," Marty Rivers muttered.

As he went roaring upward he realized how different this was from target practice and maneuvers. It was a satisfying experience. Never before had he let loose on a live target. Shooting down the big bomber had given him a strange thrill and a sort of gone feeling at the pit of his stomach.

He knew he had to let the other bombers get away because the sky was swarming with low-winged little pursuit planes, the type the Japs used on their carriers. Japan attacking the United States! This seemed crazy, but at the moment he didn't have time to consider it—not with a sky full of Japs coming down on him and every one of them in a key position.

Well, he'd show them what a Wildcat could do. He laid over on his back with the belly of his plane to the rising sun and knifed away from two darting planes. Then he went up, with the Wildcat standing on her prop, reaching for those tropical stars the sun had blotted out. He sighted O'Toole far off to his right. The Texas boll weevil had gone crazy. He was stunting in a manner that made the hornets swarming around him seem as though they were pinned to the sky. Marty grinned widely, and as he grinned his eyes were on the two Japs who had closed in on him.

Twisting into a tight spiral, he came around. His lips pulled back from his clenched teeth as he drove one Jap into his line of fire. The Jap went up, fighting for altitude, while his wing mate, taking advantage of the situation, probably was banking down below to get the Wildcat into position.

"One at a time, son," Mart muttered, and then let go at the Jap in his windscreen.

Marty winced as he saw ragged holes spreading across the fuselage and wings of the fleeing ship. He could almost feel those slugs raking the fellow up ahead. But there were dozens of the little fighters, and there were only three Wildcats. He'd better remember that before he went soft. He was reminded of it by a stream of bullets that raked around him, ripping chunks out of his wings and opening a hole close to his feet. The soft Pacific air gushed in around him as he shoved the stick and went down in a screaming dive.

There was no time for a nice long dive. Marty had to make it tight and come zooming up. The Wildcat rode upward in a terrific rush, her Wright-Cyclone motor roaring savagely. As she mounted she slowed a little, but she went high above the three little fighters darting in to cut her off.

Marty glared at the streaking hornets as they flipped past. That would give them an eyeful. As he went over he saw Captain Edwards slashing into a formation of five Japs. A long plume of smoke was trailing away behind the captain's Wildcat and the ship was riding almost on her side. He'll have to go in, Marty thought.

But the captain wasn't going in. He managed to straighten his plane and opened up on the Jap who had dived in recklessly for the kill. The little plane seemed to explode in the air. Marty shouted hoarsely as he lay over and went roaring down to help Edwards.

As he came in on the tail of a Jap and slashed it until one wing ripped loose and hurtled high above the plummeting ship, he saw that the captain's Wildcat was flaming.

"Jump! Bail out!" he bellowed into his flap mike.

As though obeying his order, a dark bundle tumbled out of the flaming coffin. A moment later Edwards' parachute blossomed into a white flare. Marty laid over and started up. As he went he saw two Japs diving toward the slowly descending parachute. Savagely he banked and went down.

"The dirty yellow dogs!" he snarled.

As he roared across the hatch cover of the nearest Jap, spraying him with lead, he had the satisfaction of seeing the other fighter duck and start climbing. Over and up he went, laying the Wildcat over on her side to see if he had rid the captain of his assassin. The Jap fighter he had raked was slithering away toward the ocean.

Marty peered down upon the island. As he looked he saw O'Toole's Wildcat going down, end over end, like a crazy bat. He waited to see if O'Toole bailed out. No white chute blossomed, and Marty gritted his teeth. O'Toole must be badly hit or caught in the wreckage of his plane. Suddenly the Wildcat below slithered sidewise, righted and leveled off just above the sand. Then it nosed down and plowed into the beach.

As he went up and over Marty saw a lank form crawl out of the wreckage and run toward the emplacements where Major Delaney's shore guns were battering away.

A feeling of relief surged through him as he sent his ship up. Both his mates were alive. But B.M.F. 213 had been reduced to one plane and that plane was more like a sieve than a trim Grumman Wildcat. Marty looked for more of the little Jap fighters and saw that they were out to sea, circling over the battlewagons offshore. He headed that way.

As he roared out over the water he noticed that there were only four battleships now. He was certain that there had been five. As he flew out he went up to get a break with the swarm of fighters. They saw him coming and zoomed in circles as he came in. Looking down, Marty saw that he was almost directly above a cruiser. He figured that she was of at least ten thousand tons. Her guns were roaring and the sea around her was filled with clouds of swirling smoke. As he eased over Marty saw she was down by the stern. The long rollers coming in to the beach were smashing over her deck. Major Delaney's boys were demonstrating their marksmanship. Then he saw the forward gun turret lift in a flash of blinding flame and go overboard.

There was no time to see more. Two Japs were on his tail, two more were coming down on him from above. How many were coming up from below, he had no way of knowing. He nosed down and caught one of the fighters squarely in his sights. His hand gripped the gun release and then jabbed the black button. Nothing happened. He was out of ammunition!

In the next few seconds Marty did a lot of stunts forbidden by the Civil Aeronautics Commission. He raked the hatch cover off a fighter who tried to head him off, and was startled to find that the Jap ship had a wooden body. Splinters and strips of dope sheet filled the air. Then he knifed down with his Cyclone roaring sweetly. Marty recalled that Japs are supposed to be suicide fliers, but he didn't find any in the sky who wanted to dispute his path to the beach.

He came inside the wall of his own anti-aircraft fire and eased down upon the sand, letting his plane roll close to a pit where five grimy and powder-stained marines were feeding a long-snouted archie. They waved at him as he tumbled out of the plane.

O'Toole and Edwards ran out to meet him. O'Toole was grinning. Edwards was as grim as ever.

"Sure, and it was some fun while it lasted," O'Toole shouted.

"Are you injured, Rivers?" Edwards snapped.

"No, but the old Wildcat is a mess. The boys

will have a lot of patching to do," Marty answered.

"The only mechanic we have left is Sergeant Emory. They got the rest when they blasted the hangar," Edwards snapped again. "We'll patch her up ourselves."

"The major's boys seem to be doing all right," Marty said.

"They sure are. A cruiser and a destroyer isn't bad at all," O'Toole answered.

Marty looked out to sea and saw only three battleships. They were circling and heading away from the island.

"Sure, and they're on the run!" O'Toole crowed.

"Come, we have a ship to patch up," Edwards barked. "Those yellow killers will be back. They aim to take this island."

"Not as long as we're here," O'Toole answered.

"No, but we won't be here very long," the captain answered grimly. "Major Delaney has just thirty men left. Those Japs have a transport full of troops just offshore."

"When is help coming?" Marty asked.

Edwards looked at him for a long minute. "Radio says Japan declared war on us. Pearl Harbor has been attacked and Manila too. There won't be any reinforcements for this post. We hold out as long as we can." He turned on his heel and headed toward the spot where the hangar had been.

Marty looked at O'Toole. O'Toole's mouth had sagged open. Marty grinned.

"So now you know what a marine is," he said softly.

"I used to be a bug exterminator. From now on I'm a Jap exterminator. Sparks, down at the radio, says those Japs landed on us long before they declared war on us. That makes exterminatin' 'em a real pleasure." O'Toole's jaw thrust out and his long neck craned upward.

"It would seem they are about to do the exterminating," Marty answered.

"We'll get our share," O'Toole growled as he turned toward the wrecked hangar where a part of the machine shop was still standing.

Marty walked along with him. He was wondering if Edwards would let him go on flying the Wildcat after she was patched up. It was his ship, but Edwards was in command. The first thing they had to do, of course, was to patch her up.

PATCHING UP the Grumman Wildcat was a tough job. Sergeant Emory salvaged as many parts from the two wrecked planes as he could. Captain Edwards' plane was almost a total loss, due to fire, but O'Toole's ship was not so badly damaged.

While the three fliers worked feverishly upon the ship, the Japs continued to batter the island with their bombers. The first wave had hardly vanished when another appeared—nine twin-motored Mitsubishi bombers flying in perfect formation. They swooped low over the island and their bombs tore great craters in the sandy beach. One

gun nest went up in a litter of debris. The marines manning the anti-aircraft guns pounded
away. O'Toole leaped to his feet and shouted
loudly when one of the bombers swung out of
line, wavered, then slid off toward the sea, black
smoke billowing out of its center section. Marty
Rivers stood and watched. Captain Edwards
went on working without even looking up.

The bombers vanished out to sea, then came
back from another angle, and again the island
rocked and craters gutted the beach. This time
the gunners got another killer and crippled a
third. But the destruction was terrible. Major
Delaney's batteries were weakened by the loss of
two five-inch guns and many men.

Edwards backed away from the ship. He
spoke to Emory. "Think we can rig her for a
bomb?" he asked.

"Yes, sir," Emory answered. "But it will be
dangerous dropping it. She might not come out
of a dive after the egg drops."

"Lend a hand and we'll make the installation,"
the captain ordered. "There happens to be a

transport out there. It is loaded with **Japs** headed for this island."

"Hurray!" O'Toole shouted. "I want the job of flying her."

Edwards said nothing. He was hurrying toward the shed where part of their supplies remained intact. Back of that shed was a pit with half a dozen bombs in it. Marty followed him with O'Toole dropping in behind.

Fitting the Wildcat out as a divebomber proved to be difficult, but Emory was a wizard at mechanics, and when he had finished even Edwards permitted himself a brief smile. The Wildcat not only looked like a bomber but she had a big bomb snuggled under her belly.

"I'd like to take her up, sir," Marty said.

"So would I," Edwards answered. "We'll toss for it." He fished out a coin. "You and I first, O'Toole." He flipped the coin into the air. "Call it."

"Heads," O'Toole said.

The coin hit the sand and Edwards bent over it. "You win." He picked up the coin. "Now you call it, Rivers." He sent the coin spinning into the air.

"Tails," Marty called.

The coin landed at his feet, spun around and lay with a shining eagle gleaming up at him.

"Too bad, O'Toole," he said with a grin.

O'Toole's face showed his disappointment but he held out a bony hand. "Here's luck."

"Let the battlewagons go. Get the transport," Edwards ordered. "Be sure you make a hit. That will mean a low dive into their guns. Just keep in mind they have a carrier lying offshore and that it will be swarming with fighters."

Marty nodded. "I'll remember."

Edwards and O'Toole helped Emory get the ship set and warmed up. Marty climbed into the outfit he had discarded. When the Cyclone was turning over sweetly he climbed aboard and pulled the hatch cover shut. He lifted a hand and the others stood clear. Kicking one wheel brake, he gave the Wildcat the gun.

Marty listened and felt for the lift of the ship, as she bounced along over the uneven sand. She came off slowly because of the added weight of the bomb and was logy on the first turn. She would be helpless if attacked in the air by Jap fighters. Circling, he headed away from the scene of action and out to sea in the opposite direction from the ships, riding well out beyond the range of shore batteries.

He let the Wildcat climb upward as fast as she could. He wanted to come down out of the sun in a screaming dive that could not be stopped by the Jap fighters. As he circled higher into the blue he spotted the transport ship. Its low black hulk lay close to the protecting destroyers so as to be shielded by their aircraft guns.

Marty craned his neck and smiled grimly. He figured he might have the element of surprise in his favor. Of course the ships were all equipped with detectors, but the Japs had planes flying and that would help confuse things.

His luck held for a time and he saw no fighter planes. He was circling high above the ships, lying offshore, when, suddenly, he sighted the carrier. She was in closer than he had thought

she would come. A few minutes later he saw
specks swirling up off her deck and around her
like hornets out of a nest. The fighters were
coming! Marty nosed over and went down the
chute. His hand gripped the make-shift release
lever Emory had rigged for him.

Down went the Wildcat, her leading-edges
screaming, her whole frame shuddering. The
deck of the transport below began to swerve upward. Marty could see tiny forms racing about
on her deck, and the guns of the three destroyers
began to lash out at him.

His ship nosed toward the field of flaming
muck spread by the guns on the battlewagons.
She hit the muck and rocked as a shell exploded
almost on top of her. Then rolling and lurching,
she went down through. Now the deck of the
transport was coming up at a sickening pace. It
was alive with soldiers, armed with rifles and
equipped with kits.

Marty gritted his teeth and took a snap chance.
He hung on for five more counts and when it
seemed he must surely smash into the deck of the

ship, he jerked the lever. The Wildcat shuddered and bounced. The release had worked! Marty pulled with all his strength and shut his eyes.

There was an air-shaking roar somewhere under his wings, and a rush of wind from the blast hurled the Wildcat upward as though she had been a chip. The explosion saved Marty from smacking into the side of one of the destroyers. He roared over her deck so close that his landing gears, still dangling, made the Jap sailors roll on the deck.

As he went up Marty had a glimpse of the transport. She was rolling over on her side and her bow was coming up at a sharp angle. Men were spilling off her decks into the water in wild confusion. Then he felt a terrific jar. Shells were screaming all around him. He put the plane into a convulsion of dips, swerves, and twists, trying to keep from giving the gunners on the destroyers a steady target.

Marty knew he still had the fighters to deal with and tried to lay over and go up. A blinding burst of fire struck through his hatch cover and seemed to explode against the instrument board. Marty felt his goggles and radio-earphones rip free from his head. He jerked his hand up over his face and instinctively sent the Wildcat into a dive.

Luck was with Marty Rivers. He dived toward land. When he was able to see again, the island was swaying toward him through his windscreen and he was diving into the muzzles of Major Delaney's guns. Lifting the ship, he eased her over and shook his head. His right arm felt numb and his right hand was a bloody mess, but he wasn't dead and the Wildcat was still flying.

Glancing back, Marty saw that the Jap fighters were roaring down on him. He wiggled the stick and started to cut back. The Wildcat failed to respond. Then as suddenly as the shellburst had hit him, flames began licking from the forward compartments and surging back into his face.

The heat was terrific, but he wasn't over the

island yet, so he went up and over, trying to shake the fire out of her. At last he gave up and palmed back what was left of the hatch cover. Clambering out like a coon from a smoking log, he dived.

The rush of cool air which suddenly hit him was soothing and cooling. Marty felt around as he let himself fall. He did not aim to blossom out until he was safe from the guns of the darting fighters who were zooming down, eager to pot him when he sailed free under his silk. Pawing, he got himself upright in the air and went down at a terrific rate, but not as fast as he had learned to take it when divebombing. As the island's sand reeled up at him he jerked the rip cord and felt the sudden jerk of his harness. In a second he was dangling there in the air. Above him a fighter plane was diving down with guns spitting. The bullets whined close to Marty and all he could do was to cringe and wait.

But the boys on the ground could do something. They centered on the diving assassin and their aim was deadly. Marty saw a shell hit the

tail section of the diving killer and blast away
everything except a few long brace lines. The
dismembered tail went kiting off to one side and
the plane nosed over, going down with that sickening dead plunge which meant the end for another Jap pilot unless he could bail out.

Marty watched the little fellow fighting to get
out. He found himself hoping the fellow would
make it. He managed to get clear and took to
his silk. A moment later he was sailing down
close to Marty. Marty grinned across at him
and shouted:

"I thought you birds were supposed to commit
suicide?"

"Next time, but not this time," the Jap called
back in perfect English.

"Happy landing!" Marty shouted.

The Jap did not answer. He was busy working his lines, trying to land at sea instead of on
the island. Marty settled down over the water
close to shore. He freed himself for the plunge,
and when the green water was close under his
boots, he cut loose from his chute and dived. The

water closed over him and he came up sputtering.

As he headed for shore he saw that the Jap flier was swimming out into the ocean, hoping to be rescued. Two marine gunners rushed down and dragged Marty up the sandy beach. He was weak and shaken and his arm was throbbing, but he refused to be carried and made it to a dugout under his own power.

A raking burst of gunfire from a diving plane kicked sand over Marty and his rescuers as they plunged over a bank and down into a dugout. Back of a cement wall three men were working on a 50-caliber machine gun. Marty grinned as he recognized Edwards, O'Toole and Emory.

"Welcome home," O'Toole sang out.

"Good going," Edwards snapped.

Marty turned and looked out over the top of the barricade. Far out in the blue the transport's bow was lifting toward the sky.

"She's going, sir," he shouted.

The four marines stood watching the troop ship rise out of the water, then slowly turn over and slide below the white-capped rim of the

ocean. The machine gun was forgotten. No one
spoke for a long time. Around them the guns
were silent except for an occasional burst in the
shallow water where the shells from the Jap destroyers were falling short.

"We have to patch this fifty up so we can
swing her overhead," Edwards finally said.
"They'll blast us out of here with bombers."

"I'll get her fixed, sir," Emory replied.

"Why do they send a whole army and navy
against an island with only forty marines on it?"
Marty asked. "Looks like a waste of material."

"We have a radio and we did have six patrol
planes. We could have spotted everything they
were doing in this part of the world," Edwards
answered grimly.

"Now, we sit here and wait for 'em to come and
get us," O'Toole drawled. "Hope they try to
land this afternoon."

"They are likely to wait until tonight." Edwards' leathery face had a pleasant, almost
pleased look on it. "You men can operate the
fifty. I believe I shall see just how rusty

I am with a Springfield rifle and a bayonet."

"The destroyers are moving off," Emory reported.

It appeared the Japs had had enough for one day. They were moving back. "You don't suppose they're running out on us?" O'Toole asked in a disappointed voice.

Marty was busy wrapping his scarf around his burned and torn hand, and Edwards noticed the wound for the first time.

"Report to the medical unit," he said. "You ought to know better than to try to patch yourself up in this climate. It crawls with every kind of disease and vermin."

"That an order, sir?" Marty asked.

"That is an order."

"Yes, sir." Marty got to his feet.

"The doc is up behind what is left of the machine shop," Emory said.

Marty clambered out of the pit and started up the sloping beach. The island was still and peaceful except for the cries of the water birds wheeling above. Smoke rose from the ruins of the barracks. A half dozen men worked over the wreckage, salvaging what they could for future use. Marty wondered how many of Major Delaney's men were left.

The hospital quarters turned out to be a canvas covered space behind one remaining wall of the machine shop. Marty stood looking at the rows of cots standing in the shade. Lieutenant Parker was working over a man laid out on a door supported by two wooden horses from the shop. He glanced up and nodded to Marty.

"Sit down, Rivers. I'm in a bit of a rush now but I'll be with you in a few minutes."

Marty sat down. There were eight men laid out on cots. The man on the operating table made nine. Marty wondered how many able marines were left. One of the men began asking for water and Marty got up to get it for him. Doctor Parker spoke to him as he lifted the water jug from beside the first aid cabinet.

"Just one cup of water, Lieutenant."

Marty nodded. He knew by the way the doctor spoke that there wasn't much water. The island's supply of fresh water came from a distillation plant which had been located just inside the hangar. This was an angle he had not thought about.

The marine on whom Doctor Parker was working was a veteran of many years' service. Marty moved over to help the doctor place him on a cot, and the wounded man grinned up at him.

"How do you feel, leatherneck?" Marty asked.

"I'll be up and at 'em tomorrow," the marine answered.

Marty forced a grin to hide the sick feeling he had at the pit of his stomach. The shell shocked soldier had no idea how badly he was smashed. Doctor Parker caught Marty's look and smiled. As they turned away from the cot he said:

"Lefty is tough. He's apt to do just what he says, that is, within a month or so." He turned to Marty. "Now let's see what you have wrapped up in that scarf."

Marty laughed. "After seeing these fellows I feel like a sissy."

The doctor unwrapped the scarf and set to

work. Within a short time he had the hand tightly bandaged. "You'll do for service," he said. "Run along."

Marty was glad to get out of the tent. He found Edwards and Major Delaney setting up headquarters in a tent just inside the grove of palms.

"Ready for duty, sir," he said.

"You did very well, Lieutenant," Delaney replied, then grinned. "Fact is, you did one heck of a good job."

"How are we fixed to hold them off?" Marty asked.

Delaney considered this for a moment. "We have sixteen men fit to fight, nine wounded, and four of your outfit able to help. That should be enough to hold on for awhile."

"We have to tie up as many ships and planes as we can," Edwards explained. "They hit us with a surprise move while talking peace under a white flag. That gives them the edge. Our battlewagons and carriers have to have time to get into action."

Marty nodded. "How about water?"

"There will be none, except for the wounded, unless Emory can patch up the distillation plant. He's working on it now."

"You will man a 50-calibre machine gun along with Lieutenant O'Toole," directed Delaney.

"May we take rifles along as side arms?" Marty asked.

Delaney grinned. "Sure, we have plenty of extra rifles."

Marty saluted and turned away. As he walked down the slope he looked around. Paris Island. Some spot to make a last stand. He wondered what the landing would be like. Oddly he thought of Custer and his stand against the Indians in Montana territory. United States marines and cavalry and infantry had been making stands at far outposts since the birth of the nation, fighting to the last man, going down with rifles roaring and the old flag flying overhead. There was a lump in his throat as he slid down into the pit where O'Toole sat beside the long-nosed 50.

"I'm beginnin' to get bored," O'Toole said and yawned. "There ain't a thing goin' on."

Marty sat down on the sand. "There will be after a bit," he said.

CORPORAL SKINNER was blowing first call, lustily and with an abandon which would have suggested the day was a holiday. Marty rolled over and dug his well hand into the sand. Suddenly he remembered there was a war on and that he was in the middle of a battle. He sat up and eased his wounded hand into a more comfortable position. Dawn had not yet come to the island, but the birds were setting up a noisy chorus which meant day was breaking.

Overhead the sky was alive with stars and their light revealed the tripod and the long snout of a 50-calibre machine gun. From beyond the gun came a deep and protesting grunt. O'Toole was waking up.

"I hardly get to sleep when that leather-necked corporal starts tooting," O'Toole growled.

Marty grinned widely. There hadn't been much sleep for anyone. Two hours on and two hours off. Nerves strained for an expected landing. Everyone ragged with thirst.

"Wonder if Skinner will be left to play taps when the yellow monkeys swarm in?" Marty asked thoughtfully.

"You think of the dumbest things," O'Toole snarled. "I aim to be here and you can make a note of that."

At that moment a man appeared. "Your breakfast, sir," he said to Marty. "The compliments of the major, and he says he's sorry you can't come in for mess."

O'Toole moved over and they stood looking down at their rations. There was a full pound of bully beef, a can of tomato juice, a stack of hard biscuit and a lemon. Marty caught up the can of tomato juice.

"Boy, is that something to look at!"

O'Toole was letting his juice trickle down his throat. He set the empty can down and smacked his lips.

"I hope they got a ton of that stuff."

Marty looked at his lemon and was about to suggest that the supply of juices might be short. The presence of the lemon was hint enough.

"I hope so," was all he said.

O'Toole tossed the lemon aside. "Never could go a lemon," he growled as he attacked his bully beef.

"Better stick it in your pocket. Later it may taste like a cold bumper of soda," said Marty tucking his lemon into his pocket.

White light, high above the island, began to dim the stars. Visibility became clearer and they could see the rest of the force moving about, limbering up stiff legs and arms. Major Delaney and Captain Edwards came down from the hospital tent.

"Fall in!" Delaney shouted.

The marines fell in with Marty and O'Toole

standing by. Twenty men and four officers. But the men snapped to attention as quickly and as perfectly as a battalion. They were tough, leathery-faced men, all of them veterans of many hard trips and many tight encounters. Delaney let his eye travel over them.

"Men, you have done well," he said grimly. "Today the element of surprise will not be with the enemy. You will hold your fire on the 5-inch guns until landing parties are within two thousand yards. Then all batteries will go into action." A thin smile cracked his lips. "Company dismissed!" he barked.

The men fell out and went back to their posts, leaving the four officers grouped on the beach.

"I am sorry to have to detail you men to a machine gun," Delaney said.

Marty and O'Toole both grinned. "It will be a pleasure, sir," Marty answered.

"You will have Sergeant Emory to help. That will not be a full crew but you should do, with a bit of management."

"I will take a place in the pits," Edwards said.

"That is not required, sir," Delaney replied.

"It is necessary," the captain growled.

"Quite so," Delaney agreed. "You and I will work a 30-calibre machine gun at Number Two pit."

The commander and the flight officers saluted Marty and O'Toole, then moved off.

"You'd think we had the Rainbow Brigade in action here," O'Toole grunted.

"We'll make the Japs think we have," Marty answered as they sank down beside their gun.

"Wonder what's keepin' 'em?" O'Toole said as looked up into the sky.

"Head wind," Marty answered. He had noted that the bombers would be bucking a head wind in coming out of the west.

A half hour passed and the sun came up in a blaze of heat and light. It beat down into the pits and Marty was soon dragging the lemon from his pocket. He took a suck and stowed it away again.

A few minutes later word was passed along the line that the radio man had picked up the sound

of approaching aircraft. Marty and O'Toole
jacked up their 50 and Emory made a last check.
Then they sat and waited for the killers.

A few minutes later they spotted the bombers
—eighteen of them, flying in precise formation
and very low. O'Toole grinned eagerly. "If
they hold that elevation we'll pot 'em like shoot-
in' fish," he muttered.

The bombers held their formation and came
drifting in. As they neared the shore they dived
down and eggs began to spray out of their bomb
bays. The lethal cargoes landed before the
bombers were over the strip of sand and within
good potting distance for the fifty. The one
archie Delaney was able to man began hammering away and split up the first wedge. Marty
and O'Toole went to work.

The air was filled with the rank smell of burning cordite and with flying sand. The earth
rocked and seemed to sway. As the fifty rapped
away savagely the gunners kept their eyes fixed
on the ships above them. One of the bombers
began to sink toward the center of the island.

"That one was ours," O'Toole crowed.

The bombers roared away and when they circled back, Marty counted only sixteen of them. This time they came over higher up and only the lone archie could reach them. After they had blasted the sandy beach and the entire slope into a churned and pocked inferno, they moved on, heading west.

The sand settled and the cordite fumes drifted away. The sun beat mercilessly down on the waste of sand. Marty climbed out of the pit.

A short broad-shouldered private crawled out of a pit that had been half filled with sand from an explosion close by. He was digging sand out of his eyes and saying things about the Japs which were not overly complimentary.

"It's a hopeless mess," he snarled. Then he got his eyes clear of sand and saw Marty. "—for the Japs," he added, then grinned.

"Right you are," Marty answered.

Major Delaney came striding along the bank, observing the damage. He halted before Marty.

"Any casualties?"

"None, sir," Marty answered. "Lieutenant O'Toole thinks he may have time to catch a few winks of sleep. He's down in the pit."

Delaney smiled. "They are poor shots, but they got the archie and two of her men." Delaney's eyes turned to ice again. "We will remain on the alert and be ready." He turned and walked away toward the hospital tent.

Marty seated himself on the edge of the pit. The sun beat upon him in his exposed position, but there was a breeze and that was better than being down in the pit where no air stirred. Sergeant Emory came up and sat with him as they sucked on lemons and watched the far rim of the ocean.

Lifting his glasses, Marty scanned the sea. Far out on the horizon he could see three ships. He passed the glasses to Emory.

"What do you make of that?"

Emory studied the ships. "Three destroyers, I'd say, sir."

"Right, you are," Marty answered. "Pass the word along while I go down and wake O'Toole."

O'Toole lay beside the 50, his mouth sagging open and rumbling snores coming from it. If he were having unpleasant dreams, the grin on his mouth did not show it. Marty bent over and shook him.

"Battle station, cotton-duster!" he snapped.

O'Toole sat up with a jerk and began clawing about him. Then he batted his eyes and grinned. "Air raid?" he asked.

"Three destroyers offshore."

O'Toole was up in a minute and peering over the cement emplacement. Marty passed over his binoculars and O'Toole studied the approaching ships.

"One wagon seems to be loaded with men and light boats," he said. "Looks like they figure to take over."

Emory returned and slid down into the pit. "The major says we are to let them come in close. He says two thousand yards."

"We have only 3-inch rifles left," Marty said, more to himself than anyone else.

"The boys won't be able to man but two of

those big babies," O'Toole said. "Looks like we got to mix it a bit."

Marty turned to Emory. "I know you're a mechanic, but how about bayonet work?"

Sergeant Emory smiled. "I've had bayonet school."

At that moment a marine slid into the pit. He had with him a light 30-calibre machine gun. Snapping a salute to Marty and O'Toole, he reported.

"The commander suggests this auxiliary weapon, sir," he said and turned and rushed away.

"That's my baby," O'Toole shouted.

"We'll man the 50, sergeant. Lieutenant O'Toole will handle the 30. When they rush us and we can no longer use the machine guns, we will go over the top and at them with our bayonets," Marty said.

O'Toole was peering over the embankment. "They don't aim to come in close enough for the 3-inch guns. They're pulling up out there."

Marty scanned the air for bombers. The landing party did not seem to be supported from the air, but the bombers might arrive before the attack was made. Far out, the destroyers had swung into line and puffs of smoke indicated they were trying a few shots at the island. Geysers of water spouted close to shore as the shells landed short. Then sheets of sand began to rise upward as the naval gunners tried to reach the trenches. The air was filled with the reverberating roars of the guns. No sound came from the shore guns of the marines.

After a bit the destroyers circled and edged in closer. Their shells began to tear up the beach around the defenders. The whole defense line was blanketed in flying sand as shells burst around the little company. The cement defense works protected Major Delaney's men as they lay huddled in their shelters waiting.

For an hour the Japs blasted away. Then four small boats put off from one of the cruisers. They were loaded with men armed with rifles and machine guns. Before heading for the beach they spread out into wide formation. Through his glasses Marty watched them. They headed in and moved quickly. As they came on the destroyers increased their barrage.

"You give the word," O'Toole said.

"Delaney will start the show off with the two 3-inch rifles," Marty answered. "Keep your eyes on those boats and see what happens."

The 50 was adjusted and Marty took over the sighting. Emory knelt behind the gun to service it. The 50 would be able to do a lot of damage at two thousand yards if he could place his shots.

"Wish I'd taken over the 50," O'Toole growled. "You birds will get all the pot shooting." He had shoved half of his lemon into one cheek where it bulged out like a duck egg.

The boats came on and Marty noted that four more were being lowered and shoved off. The new landing party was dividing. Two boats were moving north and two south in a wide flanking movement.

"Those babies will land outside our range," O'Toole growled. "The yellow monkeys."

Marty was following the boat moving up on

the outside. That would be his target. He set his elevation at two thousand yards and made his calculations. When the boat reached the spot he had in mind he expected Delaney to open up. His calculations did agree with those of the men on the 3-inch guns. The ground shook as the marines opened up, and a pall of smoke billowed over the pits to their right.

Marty cut loose with the 50 but he also kept an eye on the two boats at the north end of the line. One second before the guns opened up they were bobbing along, white foam rolling from their prows. A second later both had exploded in a welter of foam and broken wood and flying men. The boat Marty was concentrating on did not explode but it swung halfway around and rocked furiously. Many of the men aboard dived over the side. The fourth boat came on and Marty turned his gun on it. He was too late. Both the 3-inch rifles had swung over and opened up. The target blew up under Marty's sights.

"That peashooter ain't in class with the 3-inch ladies," O'Toole shouted.

Marty said nothing. He was watching the Jap soldiers. As they spilled into the water they started to swim toward the shore.

"They all have air jackets to float them," he said.

"Looks like duck season has opened," O'Toole answered.

The water was. alive with bobbing yellow men who were headed for shore. Marty figured that, out of the four crews, about fifty men had escaped alive and were coming on for a landing. This would not be a serious landing party. It was the four boats making the flanking movement that had to be reckoned with. They were moving far along the shore to the north and south. The 3-inch rifles had divided their fire but they could not reach the boats.

"They'll make a landing on each side of us," Marty said.

"Reckon there'll be about sixty in each herd," O'Toole said. "Still ain't enough to bother us."

The barrage from the ships suddenly ceased

but the marines did not ease their fire. It was now a matter of hammering at single targets. Machine guns and rifles joined the 3-inch guns. The Japs in the water had a sorry time. But they came on in a perfect demonstration of suicide attack.

Soaked with sweat, and grim faced, the marines picked off the invaders. Only four men reached the beach and they went down like ten pins under the concentrated fire from the trenches. But on either side the boats were making landings. Yellow men were pouring over the sides of the boats and splashing to shore.

The order came down the line to spread for attack by land. Marty and Emory got set to swing the 50 around to cover the machine shop and the beach. O'Toole dragged his thirty up into place and squatted behind it.

"Did you ever get that water gadget fixed?" he croaked as he spat out the sucked lemon from his cheek.

"No, sir," Emory answered. "It was beyond repair."

O'Toole grunted and licked his lips. Marty watched the landing party to the south. The Japs were spreading out. They had light machine guns and rifles with bayonets fixed.

"This will be duck soup," O'Toole grunted.

As they set themselves five men slid into the trench beside them.

"Reporting for bayonet attack, sir," a corporal said.

"Lie low and wait for orders. Use your rifles to pick off as many as you can."

"Six more boats are putting off," Emory reported.

"This may be the zero hour, but I'm as hot as a pickaninny in a cotton patch," O'Toole said as he mopped sweat out of his eyes.

The situation wasn't as bad as it might have been. The marines had the advantage of cover from prepared positions, and the landing parties were not well coordinated. Those on the beach were not waiting for the six boats making a frontal attack. The three inch guns would blast them well out in the surf.

"Hey, have a look!" O'Toole shouted.

Marty looked up into the air. Two formations of bombers were dropping down out of the sun. Twelve Mitsubishis were coming in very low, flying in two wedges. As they came over the destroyers they nosed down for the attack.

"Heck of a way to do us," O'Toole snarled. "Spoiling a good fight this-a-way."

Marty and Emory were busy jacking up the fifty for a whack at the bombers. Marty shot a few words at O'Toole out of the corner of his mouth.

"You take over the rifles. We'll do what we can with the bandits."

The bombers came low over the trenches, diving down until the thunder of their motors drowned out the clatter of the machine guns and the roar of the 3-inch rifles. Marty picked a Mitsubishi that was diving directly upon their position. He opened up and had the satisfaction of seeing the bomber swerve and kite over on her side, then zoom upward, spilling her eggs on the sand behind them.

But the other bandits showered the positions of the marines and rocked the ground, tearing the trenches into great pits and raising terrible havoc. When the sand settled Marty knew that the game was about over. The two 3-inch rifles were no longer blasting away. Out in the surf four boats came on at a fast pace, while a thin line of Japs charged across the sand, closing in on each side. O'Toole was ripping away at them with the machine gun and the rifles of the five men cracked steadily. The Jap lines thinned but came on.

Marty was turning the 50 on them when a hand dropped on his arm. He turned and looked into the powder smeared face of Major Delaney.

"Take Lieutenant O'Toole and Sergeant Emory and get the Sikorsky down on the far side of the island." The Major handed Marty a leather case. "These reports are to be delivered to the Marine Command at Manila." Delaney's words were bitten off sharply.

"How about Captain Edwards, sir?" Marty asked.

"The captain is wounded."

"Is this an order, sir? Do we have to run out?" Marty asked.

"It is an order and I expect you to carry it out, at once," Delaney snapped.

"Yes, sir. Do you have men to man these guns, sir?"

"No," Delaney answered.

O'Toole was standing up, his face twisted into a bleak frown. There was something more than sweat on his cheeks.

"Let me stay here, sir. I haven't had a chance to use my bayonet, Major."

"You heard my orders. It will take the three of you to get away. If you don't obey at once, you won't be able to make it!" Delaney glared at O'Toole.

"Yes, sir," O'Toole answered and shoved out a big hand. Good luck, sir—"

They shook hands with Major Delaney. As they scrambled over the bank and dived up the shore toward the machine shop, Marty heard O'Toole snarling and mumbling to himself. He glanced back and saw that Delaney was leading ten marines in a bayonet charge upon the Japs coming up from the south. That was to cover their escape. To the north a machine gun was blasting away at the party coming down from the north. That meant that there were only a few men left to support the right wing, with none to face the sea attack. A lump rose in Marty's throat as he hurried along.

At the edge of the palm grove the three airmen halted and looked back. Delaney and his men had contacted the Japs and a furious battle was on.

"They're goin' to rout 'em!" O'Toole shouted.

Marty joined the shout. The ten marines were putting the Japs to flight and swinging around to meet the attack from the north.

MAJOR DELANEY had planned for just the sort of trouble that had overtaken Eleven 13. He had cleared a pathway through the palm grove and down upon the beach. There was a steep sloping run down to a narrow lane of water hemmed in by reefs and coral ridges.

Sergeant Emory went into action the moment the three fliers reached the Sikorsky, which was always kept in readiness except for warming up her two motors. She was an S–43 model that had seen plenty of service—a dependable old crate but no fighter. Marty checked her tanks while O'Toole checked and readied her two guns.

Marty swung down and stood looking up at Emory who was working on the port motor. Emory was concentrating on his job, his mouth screwed up into a tight line.

"If the old crate weren't loaded up with instruments and observation gadgets, we could take off most of the wounded," Marty said.

Emory paused and looked down. He had been thinking the same thing. "I could jerk all of that stuff out in a hurry, sir," he said eagerly.

"O'Toole!" Marty shouted.

O'Toole's head poked out of the forward compartment. "What's up?" he called.

"I'm going to the edge of the woods to have a look. You and Emory jerk out all of the observation, weather and detector equipment. I'll be back in a few minutes. Have the engine tuning up."

O'Toole grinned eagerly. "We could take off a few of the boys from Parker's tent house," he called down.

"We sure could," Marty agreed.

"Be a violation of orders and if we got caught

by the Japs, Delaney would shoot us before sundown." O'Toole's grin was widening.

"I'll be back in a minute." Marty turned and dashed to the edge of the woods.

Peering out over a clump of palmetto, he saw that Major Delaney and his men were surrounded. They had taken refuge in a deep pit and were blasting away at a ring of Jap soldiers. Their machine guns and rifles were taking a heavy toll but Marty saw that they would be overpowered in a very short time. He looked down toward the tent shelter behind the machine shop wall. He could reach it without being seen if he had a little luck.

Turning back toward the Sikorsky, he climbed up and lent a hand in ripping loose the instrument panels. "Delaney is holding them off. Heave this stuff out and then we'll make a run for the shelter."

It took better than twenty minutes to dump all of the instruments out. Marty, O'Toole and Emory ran to the edge of the woods. They paused to look down upon the battle. Delaney and his boys were coming out of the pit with fixed bayonets to sell themselves as dearly as they could. O'Toole started to shout but Marty clapped a hand over his mouth.

"Head for Doc Parker's shelter," he snapped as he led the charge down the slope. Doctor Parker saw them coming and waved. They plunged under the shelter beside him.

"How many can we move?" Marty demanded.

"I have just six men who are alive," Parker answered.

"Can we get them up to the Sikorsky? We have orders to take off." Marty clipped the words off short.

"Do you have orders to evacuate the wounded?" Parker asked.

"Sure," O'Toole broke in. "We're giving the orders."

Parker smiled. "Fine. We should carry the cots up there."

"We can take two. That will mean three trips. Let's get going." Marty bent toward the nearest cot.

"These two first," Parker ordered.

They moved out of the shelter and up the slope, bending low, hoping the Japs would be too busy to see them. Reaching the Sikorsky, they placed the cots inside. Marty let down two ship's bunks and O'Toole fixed two more. That would care for them.

They raced back to the shelter for two more wounded men. On their way up they noticed that the firing below had slackened. Within a few minutes the Japs below would be able to hear the motors of the Sikorsky. They did not load the men aboard but hurried back for the last two.

There was a delay on the last trip while Parker gathered his kit of supplies and placed it on one of the cots. The wounded marine on the cot grinned up at Marty.

"You're going for a ride, leatherneck," Marty said.

"Good," the man replied. "But I'd rather be out there having a whack at those yellow monkeys."

As they picked up the cots the shooting below stopped and they could hear the motors of the Sikorsky.

"Make a dash for it," Marty ordered.

They caught up the cots and dashed away. As they left the shelter of the wall they heard men shouting below and rifles cracking. The sand lifted all around them and Marty was glad few Jap soldiers could see to shoot accurately above two hundred yards. He glanced back and saw a squad of Japs charging up the slope.

Dashing into the palms, they loaded the two cots and transferred the men to the ship's bunks. Then the two outside were transferred. Marty and O'Toole took their places at the controls. Emory manned the rear gun while Parker stood close beside the cots.

"Thumbs up!" Marty shouted as he gave the motors the gun.

The Sikorsky's Platt and Whitney motors roared; and the ship shuddered and began to break free. Marty felt, rather than heard, the bullets of the charging Japs as they slapped into the ship. The Sikorsky seemed to be getting into action slowly. She nosed ahead and dipped down the sandy runway toward the open lane of water. In the rear Emory was slamming away with the rear gun, picking off the charging Japs who were almost upon the plane.

They slid away, gaining speed, and soon outdistanced the charging infantry. The Sikorsky hit the water at three times the regulation speed. She bucked and rocked and jumped but kept on gaining speed. Myriads of wading birds rose from the bordering coral reefs and swarmed into the air. Marty steadied the big ship and opened her wide up for the take-off.

"Bombers coming back over," O'Toole reported. "I'll take over the forward gun."

Marty grinned and nodded. Here was where the old Sikorsky proved she was a fighting ship as well as a utility craft. He felt her begin to lift, smash a lower roller, then lift free. Slowly she skimmed out over the ocean, gaining speed and lifting slowly, her Hornets droning powerfully.

As they swung around to head west, Marty
looked down upon the island. A little group of
marine stood in line facing a large body of Japanese troops. He was glad he was so far up
that he could not see the scene clearly. Savagely
Marty Rivers laid the Sikorsky over and headed
her toward Manila.

Two of the bombers left formation and
wheeled back to give chase to the escaping Sikorsky. As they droned into line Emory
opened fire upon them while O'Toole fumed and
growled because he could not get his gun into
action. Marty eased the Hornets wide open
and coaxed the big ship to deliver her last ounce
of power. He had desperately wounded men
aboard and could do no stunts.

The two Mitsubishi bombers trailed for a few
miles and Marty began to smile grimly. The
Sikorsky was showing them her heels in pretty
fashion. Marty made a note to report that.
Those Jap bombers were not over fast. Presently they dropped away astern and wheeled

back toward Paris Island. O'Toole came back and sank into the seat beside him.

"I'm so dry I could drink Texas slough water," he muttered.

"Parker might be able to spare a drink around. We ought to be in within six hours," Marty suggested.

O'Toole went back and returned a few minutes later with a canteen. "Parker donated this. He's so glad to get his cripples out of the clutches of those Japs that he would have donated his shirt."

Marty looked ahead into blue space as he tipped up the canteen and filled his mouth with water. It was bitter and warm but it had no salt in it and moistened the inside of his mouth. Lowering the canteen, he looked across at O'Toole.

"How do you feel?"

"Like a rat," O'Toole answered sourly. "Didn't you look down on the island as we came over?"

Marty nodded. "And we'll make the Japs pay for that cleanup, a hundred times over."

O'Toole's homely face was deadly and he looked straight ahead toward the west.

"Just load me with bombs and head me for Tokio, that's all I ask," he stated.

Emory came forward for instructions and Marty sent him back to his post at the rear gun.

"No telling when we'll plow into a flight of fighters. The nearer we get to base the more likely we are to hit trouble. As you go back try to contact the naval base and tell them we are coming in. The boys might lend us a hand, just in case."

"Just in case they're not too busy," O'Toole broke in.

"Yes, sir, I'll report back," Emory said.

Marty made a few calculations and changed his course a little. He had flown this leg of the Trans-Pacific route several times before but never without full instrument help. After a time Emory came forward and reported:

"They say to come on in. The base has been bombed and there's heavy fighter action right now. No planes available to cover our landing. We are to take our chances." Emory saluted and stood waiting.

"Lay off the radio unless I call for a report," Marty said. "The less we broadcast, the better."

An hour went by and Parker came forward to get O'Toole to help him with one of the men. The doctor was in high spirits. Marty grinned at him.

"You have a lot of faith in our being able to drop you safely in the bay," he said.

"You'll make it, Lieutenant," Parker answered.

O'Toole stayed back with the doctor for the next hour. When he returned Marty handed over the controls while he eased his injured hand and arm.

"Hold her on the marked course by the compass," he said.

O'Toole nodded as he took over. **Marty lay**

back with his arm supported. At first he thought he would doze off, but discovered he could not even close his eyes.

O'Toole flew the Sikorsky for the next two hours when Marty took over again so that he could go forward to man the gun. They were coming in and might have a bit of trouble. As they swept inland over the thrusting tip of Luzon Marty sighted fires far ahead. The smoke was black and had pillared high into the sky. He knew those were oil fires. The Japs must have hit an oil depot. Sliding out over Manila Bay, he looked down at the city. It seemed to be peaceful enough.

Two P–40's ripped past and their pilots gave him the lucky sign. Marty wondered if they had heard the story of Paris Island. Later a Martin bomber roared past them loaded with bombs and bristling with armament. They saw no Jap fighters as they settled down. Marty called Emory on the inter-com telephone and put him at the radio. A few minutes later he caught the signals coming up to the Sikorsky.

"Sikorsky from Marine Aircraft Group, Eleven 13, come in."

"Sikorsky from Marine Aircraft Group, Eleven 13, coming in," Marty answered into his flap-mike.

The amphibian dropped in, circled and hit the low rollers smoothly. A few minutes later they were taxiing up to a float. A dozen sailors appeared and made them fast. Marty palmed his hatch door and looked out.

"Hi, leatherneck," an ensign called up to him. "How is the weather in Paris?"

"Hot," Marty answered and grinned.

The ensign's smile faded. "How many did you bring in?"

"Six wounded men and four able bodied men," Marty answered.

The ensign nodded. He did not have to ask what had happened to the others. O'Toole was eager to get out so they climbed down and the sailors turned in to help Doctor Parker. Marty waited for Emory. The three of them would make the report.

They walked up the plank and across the dock toward the office of the commander. Marty led the way into the office. A grayhaired man sat at a desk. He rose and saluted them.

"Sit down, gentlemen," he said.

"I have a report, sir, from Major Delaney commanding at Paris Island," Marty said as he laid the leather folder on the commander's desk.

Colonel Keller opened the case and turned the soiled reports over one at a time. His face did not change expression as he read. When he had finished he put the reports down very gently and looked up.

"My compliments, gentlemen," he said.

O'Toole swallowed a couple of times. "We hated to run out on them, sir."

The colonel looked at him for a moment before saying: "A marine obeys orders, sir."

"We wish immediate service, sir," Marty said.

The colonel's somber frown changed to a smile. He looked the three bedraggled and soiled fliers over with a critical eye.

"You need a rest and some food," he said.

"However, your Sikorsky will be held in readiness for you."

"We want to stay right here and be assigned to Grumman Wildcats," O'Toole broke in. "I want a crack at those Japs."

"The personnel may have to be shifted to a point south of here," the colonel said. "In the meantime, after you have cleaned up and rested a day, we may be able to find planes for you."

"You mean we'll have to get out of the Philippines?" Marty asked.

"That is not our plan at the moment, but we do not have enough fighter strength to last very long," the colonel answered.

Marty stared at him. This was terrible. He had thought Manila would be like getting back to the U.S.A.—a safe spot from which to operate.

"I know what you're thinking," the colonel said. "You feel that if a handful of marines on Paris Island could do so much damage to the Japs, we ought to be able to do a lot more here. But it will be worse here and we will have more trouble. The Japs will make landings, I'm afraid. Now go along and get something to eat and drink."

The three fliers stood up and saluted. They went out into the hot sunshine and O'Toole gave vent of his feelings.

"What kind of a war is this, anyway? Those Japs can't push us around."

"You heard what the colonel said," Marty answered.

CHAPTER 5 DIVEBOMBER

MARTY AND O'TOOLE reported to the marine officer in charge of Operations after O'Toole had located a canteen and had finished off seven bottles of iced pop. The dark-eyed little Philippino girl behind the counter watched, fascinated while O'Toole tipped up the seventh bottle. The bottle had remained tipped until the last drop of strawberry pop trickled down the boll weevil's lanky throat. With a sigh he set the bottle down.

"Another?" the girl asked timidly.

O'Toole sighed again and shook his head. "After we report in, sweetheart, I'll be back for a drop more. Right now I have to be careful not to overtax me starved body."

Marty laid a dollar on the counter. "Keep the change," he said with a grin.

"Thank you, sir," the girl said. "But I'd rather not. If I could do it I'd not charge you anything."

Marty laughed. "You're all right, but the marines have no use for money." He shoved the dollar across to her and turned away.

O'Toole looked longingly at the gay posters depicting ice cream sodas and huge malted milks heaped high and overflowing with icy foam.

"It's here I'd like to stay," he said.

"You can come back," Marty said impatiently. "I want to report in before they run out of fighter planes."

"I reckon you're right," O'Toole agreed.

They walked across to the Marine Operations Room and entered. The place was deserted except for a captain seated behind a tall desk. He was busy working on a pile of reports and did not look up. Marty and O'Toole crossed the

room.   O'Toole leaned his elbows on the desk
and greeted the captain.

"We came over to check out a couple of Wildcats."

The captain looked up and stared at them.
"Where have you two been for the last couple
of days?" he growled sourly.

"Paris Island," Marty answered.   "And we're
short of equipment."

The captain's eyes opened wider.   "Are you
what is left of Eleven 13?" he asked slowly.

"We are that," O'Toole answered.   "And we
got a lot of scores to even up."

The captain laid aside his pencil and rubbed
his hand over his hair.   He continued to look
the boys over carefully.   Finally he nodded and
pulled out a pad from a slot in the desk.   Picking up his pencil, he poised it above the paper.

"We reported in and delivered papers from
Major Delaney," Marty explained.

The captain suddenly bent forward.   "How
did it go?" he asked.

"Lousy," O'Toole answered.   "Before we

knew there was a war on, a flock of bombers came over and blasted our reserve Wildcats. We went up and knocked off a few but the air was so full of Kariganes that we just naturally couldn't shove 'em out of the sky."

"What about Delaney and the boys?"

"We were ordered out with dispatches," Marty said simply.

The captain's eyes glittered. "Delaney handed them something, I'll bet on that."

"Two destroyers, one transport, and a few hundred Japs got really wet," Marty answered.

The captain smiled. "Good," he said, and then his face became grim again. "Here I sit poking a pencil at a pile of reports, it's a rotten break. Delaney always was a lucky stiff."

Marty nodded. He was thinking of a ragged and powder-blackened little squad standing on a patch of blistering sand with a ring of Jap bayonets around them. Lifting his eyes to the trim, neatly pressed uniform of the captain, he said.

"Do we get a couple of Wildcats?"

"Fighter planes are about as easy to get as they were on your island. We figure our combat line will be able to hold out a few days longer." He studied the grimy marines across the desk from him. "But I do have one Douglas S.B.D.I. I can assign. It's been spoken for but I figure you boys deserve another crack at those yellow rats."

"Thanks," Marty answered.

"You can team up on that divebomber. I'll fix up your orders and clearance and send them over to operations. How long are you grounded for repairs?"

"One day, countin' today," O'Toole said eagerly.

"One day, counting tomorrow," the Captain answered. "You birds are making fools of yourselves. I have to crack down or every man in the outfit will be flying twenty-four hours a day."

"We don't need any rest," O'Toole growled.

The captain smiled. "I'm not thinking of you leatherheads, I'm thinking of the planes. Every time a pilot drops off to sleep it saves the Japs a round of ammunition."

When Marty and O'Toole reported to barracks they discovered there was nothing on the quartermaster's shelves in the way of fresh clothing so they headed for the shower room. With water pelting him, O'Toole shouted:

"Boy, am I hungry! Hope they're not out of food."

"We'll soon find out," Marty answered.

Rubbing down briskly, they got into their torn and soiled uniforms and headed toward the mess. Here they found several flight lieutenants at the traditional coffee table, who got up at once when Marty and O'Toole entered. A lanky youth with a shock of blond hair rushed forward.

"Marty, you tramp!" he shouted.

"Bill Chester!" Marty gripped Bill's hand. "This is my partner, Mike O'Toole," he said as he stepped back.

Bill Chester introduced the other fliers and they all sat down. O'Toole wrinkled his nose.

"I reckon I'll eat," he said.

"Sure, you'll eat," Bill answered and shouted. "Corporal!"

While the corporal was taking their orders the fliers fired questions at Marty and O'Toole.

"We'll outfit you," Bill assured them when he learned they were without a change of clothing.

Silently they listened while Marty told of the fight on Paris Island. O'Toole devoted himself to his meal, refusing to talk until he had eaten a steak and a whole berry pie.

"We'll even this up," Bill said. "The marines can't be pushed around that way."

"We will if we ever get any planes," one of the men answered. "I'm about to join one of MacArthur's gun crews."

"We got us an S.B.D.I.," O'Toole said and beamed.

Marty kicked his shin under the table. They had been given preference over these boys and it might not sit well. Bill Chester spoke up at once.

"You earned it. But you better take care of

that crate. When she's down you sit around and swill coffee."

The other fliers nodded. None of them showed any resentment, though they did envy the luck of the two boys from Paris Island.

"How about uniforms?" Bill asked.

The other men joined in with offers of clothing. Marty and O'Toole went with the men and soon were trim and neat as though getting set for a parade.

"I reckon I'll take a nap," O'Toole said. "You-all run along and play."

"How about you, Marty?" Bill asked.

"I better turn in, too," Marty said. "That dinner made me sleepy. We kept pretty late hours on the island."

After the boys left them Marty did not go to sleep for a long time, but O'Toole was snoring within five minutes. Marty considered the news they had heard of operations on Luzon. He was sure MacArthur would be no push-over. He knew the general well and admired him greatly. But without air support there might be serious trouble. A flight of bombers droned overhead and within a few minutes Marty heard fighter planes screaming. He could tell by the whine of their motors that there weren't many of them. Restlessly he turned over and tried to shut out the sounds. Finally his tired body demanded rest and he fell asleep.

Marty woke up with sun shining in through a high window and laying a yellow band across the floor. Yawning, he raised himself on one elbow. From the direction of the sun's rays he could tell it was late afternoon; and he must have slept all day. Swinging his feet to the floor, he looked across at O'Toole.

The boll weevil lay on his back with his mouth open. He was snoring lustily. Marty reached over and gripped one lanky bare foot. With a yank he jerked O'Toole off onto the floor. The boll weevil landed with a thud. He came up instantly with his long arms flailing out and his hands balled into fists.

"Come on, you yeller rat!" he bellowed.

"Up and at 'em!" Marty shouted.

O'Toole blinked as he let his arms drop. "Is that any way for you-all to treat a pal?" he asked sourly.

"We've overslept," Marty explained.

"I reckon we have at that. I'm hungry as a bear." O'Toole ran his finger through his mop of red hair. "Reckon I'll have a steak for breakfast with a side order of kidneys, then I'll have me regular bacon and eggs." He grinned up at Marty.

"Just a snack?" Marty asked.

"I don't aim to overload me stummick," O'Toole explained.

"Let's get going. If you plan to spend a couple of hours eating we may lose our chance to grab that Douglas Defiant." Marty began getting into his tropical outfit.

Since it was early for the dinner hour the mess was deserted. O'Toole had to do without his kidneys but he got his steak and a big order of bacon and eggs. Marty finished eating long before his pal had started on his bacon and eggs, and sat back and waited. O'Toole devoured his breakfast and then looked toward the kitchen.

"I might have just a small slab of pie," he ventured.

"If you order another bite of grub, I'm leaving you here," Marty warned.

O'Toole sighed as he rose. "You don't appreciate grub when you can get it."

They crossed the grounds and entered the operations room. The same captain was seated behind the tall desk. He looked weary and out of sorts. At first he did not recognize them dressed in natty uniforms. He snapped:

"No assignments up. No pursuit planes available."

"How about that Douglas Defiant?" Marty asked.

The captain blinked and then smiled. "Oh, it's you tramps from the island. I saved that ship for you. Almost had to fight a duel with a major from over at Cavite."

"What's the assignment?" O'Toole asked.

"There is none. You go back and plant yourselves on a cushion at the barracks. I'll do the calling." He looked at Marty. "You flew out of here before going to Paris, didn't you?"

"I certainly did," Marty said. "I know my way about."

"Fine. We have scouting planes out. If naval units are spotted you'll have a chance to drop a few eggs."

"Thank you, sir," Marty said.

"We'll be right over there," O'Toole promised.

When they left the office O'Toole headed for the canteen. Marty went along, but he grumbled about it.

"If you make us miss a job with your thirsty gullet I'll knock your ears down."

"Just a drop of strawberry pop. I'm dry as a salted herring," O'Toole said.

After O'Toole's fourth bottle Marty turned away. "I'm heading for the barracks. You come along when the supply of pop runs out."

"I'm coming," O'Toole called after him.

By the time Marty reached the barracks O'Toole had overtaken him.

"The trouble with you is you want to rush this war. You-all can't seem to take it easy like. The old man says we aren't likely to run out of Japs," O'Toole grumbled.

They sat down in the officers' mess and waited. A half hour passed and finally an orderly appeared. He came across the room and halted before Marty and O'Toole.

"Lieutenant Rivers?" he asked.

Marty nodded. The orderly handed him a slip of paper and turned about. Marty opened the order. It was signed by Colonel Keller and ordered them to report for duty at four the next morning.

"Heck!" O'Toole muttered.

"We go another night's sleep," Marty said.

"Hear that mess call?" O'Toole asked. "I'm going to bed as soon as I have me supper."

"Supper? Why, you just got through eating a breakfast large enough for a squad."

"I'm not as hungry as I was at breakfast time, but I'll have to have a snack to carry me through," O'Toole explained.

"Just what would you consider a snack?" Marty asked.

"Well, I smell roast lamb. I'll have a helping of that and a pie. Nothing else."

"Go ahead. I'm going to take a stroll before the sun goes down. I'll see you at the room later." Marty rose and turned toward the door.

"When I feel the need of exercise I always lie down till it wears off," O'Toole said. "No use over workin'." He turned toward the mess room with a shake of his head.

The night was oppressively warm even after the sun had dipped into the South China Sea. Across the bay at Corregidor Fortress an anti-aircraft gun was whacking away. Otherwise peace and quiet reigned. As Marty swung along he wondered how the authorities could tell friend from foe among the inhabitants. It seemed to him that a fourth of the crowd moving on the streets were Japanese. A small cluster of them stood at a corner. They watched him approach and pass. As soon as he was past they began chattering in a singsong chorus.

Marty looked back and the chattering ceased. As he moved on he had an uneasy feeling.

After walking two hours Marty returned to the barracks. He found O'Toole sound asleep, lying on his back with his mouth open. In the humid heat, the boll weevil had tossed aside everything and his skinny frame was exposed. Marty wondered how any man could eat so much and still resemble a skeleton. He undressed and lay down.

THE DOUGLAS DEFIANT was trembling with restrained power, awaiting her pilot and bombardier. The ground crew had clambered down from her cockpit after warming up her radial motor. The glare of her exhaust sent shadows flickering over the oil-soaked ground.

Dusky figures loomed nearby, men dressed in light clothing or almost no clothing at all. The air was heavy, damp and warm. Marty took his flight orders from the ground officer and tucked them into his flying suit. Behind him O'Toole muttered and grumbled. He had no

98

desire to fly where he was anything but the man at the controls.

"Battlewagons sighted off Vigan coast," the officer said. "You are to pick a battleship if possible. If you don't spot a battleship or a carrier then take what you can get."

Marty saluted and said, "Call letter K for landing."

"Correct," the officer answered. "Light will hit about the time you are over the selected zone."

Marty waited for O'Toole to climb in behind, then got in and palmed his hatch cover forward. He peered out on both sides and connected his headset to listen.

"Douglas Defiant, China Sea Raid, ready?"

"Ready, sir," Marty answered as he cuddled his flap-mike.

He depressed one wheel brake and slammed the throttle knob up, snapping the Defiant around hard and sending her lurching away. A mobile floodlight poked a long finger of white light down the field. Its driver set the bar for the take-off. Marty nosed the Defiant into the beam and waited for the take-off signal from the shaded lamp of the field officer.

Bending forward, Marty checked his temperature and gauges. This was his first flight with a Defiant on a deadly mission. Many times he had gone down the glory chute to unload upon a dummy target. This would be the real thing and he wasn't flying a Wildcat patched over into a bomber.

The clearance flash came from the darkness. Marty hoiked the Defiant's tail with a blast of prop pressure and they headed down the shadow lane. The Defiant lifted and was off in a screaming roar, sweeping over the dark form of the truck with the lights, and boring upward. Back in the rear cockpit O'Toole was over his grouch and humming a Texas coon hunting tune.

They swept up over the blacked-out city of Manila, climbing steadily. Marty had a feeling he wanted to join O'Toole in his coon hunting ditty. After they left the city they swept up over a wide valley, hammering along at cruising speed. Below them was blackness with only a few lights winking. Over them arched the dome of the sky filled with big, bright stars. Somewhere to the north a convoy of Jap ships was moving in to try for a landing on the coast.

By the time they had passed Lingayen, gray light was revealing the terrain below and the stars were fading out. Marty went up a few thousand feet and called back to O'Toole.

"Keep a sharp eye out for ships."

"I'm lookin'," O'Toole answered lazily.

It was Marty who sighted the low-riding spots on the horizon of the China Sea. Far ahead he saw a wraith of smoke and below it a dark mass of objects.

"Japs ahead," he called cheerily into the intercom phone.

"Let's get at 'em!" O'Toole shouted. He was suddenly very much awake.

"Hang on, here we go!" Marty shouted as he began to build up altitude, setting the Defiant upon a great circle.

The ship moved up and circled around to hit

the Japs from the north. Below them four big cruisers and six transports plowed along, churning the placid sea into white foam. Marty laid over and looked down. There wasn't a battle-wagon in the convoy, but there was one cruiser which looked bigger and heavier than the others. It was plowing along inside a protecting line formed by the three lighter cruisers. Marty picked it as his target.

"Peeling off!" he called. "We'll take the big one on the inside. Get set for action!"

"Peel!" O'Toole growled back. "And keep your ears cleaned out while I give you a bead on the big one."

The Defiant laid over and nosed down. "Right!" O'Toole hissed. "Left! Left! Hold it!"

"Keep your shirt on. We'll go down and leave our card with the admiral," Marty drawled out of the side of his mouth.

The Defiant went down, screaming, shuddering as she gained speed. Marty held her on the target and let her dive. The sea, the transports and the cruisers lifted and seemed to float up to meet them. The deck of the cruiser grew larger and Marty checked his speed. He could see men running about on the deck. The guns below opened up and the air rocked with bursting shells.

"Right!" O'Toole shouted.

Marty eased over. A bursting shell close to the right wing had shoved him off the target.

The deck was swinging up at them, hurtling into their faces. The big bomb swung free and the Defiant shot upward as though bounced off a rubber mat. Shells screamed around them and a gaping hole appeared in the right wing. The wing surface around the hole peeled back, flapped a few times, then vanished leaving the bones of the wing revealed.

Marty laid over as they went up. He looked down upon the results of their shot. A great sheet of flame and smoke had blotted out the deck of the cruiser. He could see debris rising above the billowing smoke. It dropped back into the black pall as the smoke mounted.

"Not bad," O'Toole was crowing. "But can't you get up a bit higher. Something that felt like a shell just tickled my tummy."

The guns below were doing their best to end the career of the divebomber. Shells burst all around her, fire and flame licked at her, and she was rocked from side to side. Marty held his breath waiting for the lucky shot that would mark up a hit for the Jap gunners.

The Defiant nosed on up and burst out of the blazing muck. She seemed to shake herself as she leveled off. Marty leaned forward and re-laxed. He discovered that the insides of his hands were moist and that sweat had broken out on his forehead.

"How about plastering them with the rest of the load?" O'Toole was drawling.

"Going down!" Marty sang out.

Again they went down the chute into the muz-zles of the Jap guns. This time Marty picked a transport for the lighter bombs.

The blazing muck swallowed them and tracers threaded around them. In a few seconds they were through the blanket of fire and nosing down upon a crowded deck. The Japs seemed to have the transports packed as full of men as possible, even to the decks. O'Toole cut loose with a whoop. Marty pulled the Defiant up so close to the loaded deck that he caught a glimpse of yellow faces. He saw a great geyser of water lift just below the bomber's tail.

"Missed clean," O'Toole groaned.

"We still have our guns," Marty called back. "Get set for strafing."

They went over and came down again, raking the deck of a transport again and again. O'Toole called up to Marty:

"Don't know what's holdin' the tail on. They must have put an extra dab of glue in this job."

Marty looked back and saw that their tail assembly was all but shot away. He eased over and went up, heading toward home. As they lifted he sighted two other bombers, Army, Douglas twin-motored jobs, coming in for an attack. He also noticed that the cruiser was listing badly to port and that her crew was abandoning her. That was one for the boys back on Paris Island.

They wobbled in over Manila with the tail flapping and vibrating but hanging on. Marty set the Defiant down smoothly and taxied her up to the line. The ground crew raced out with Emory leading them. A whoop went up from the men when they saw the damage.

"Good work!" Emory called up as Marty climbed out. "You have set a record, sir, in getting her in."

"The commander wants to see you men," the field officer said as Marty and O'Toole faced him.

Marty nodded and grinned but O'Toole glared at the officer. Here they were in from a single-handed attack upon a convoy, with one cruiser sunk, and this captain of marines acted peeved because they had gotten badly shot up.

"Wonder what a guy has to do to get a medal around here?" he muttered as he followed Marty into the briefing room for their report.

Captain Midford looked up from his usual pile

of papers. Marty had an odd feeling that Midford hadn't left that pile of papers since the time they had reported to him. He didn't appear to have moved at all. He nodded to them.

"Flight two thirteen reporting in," Marty said as he piled his chute and gear on the floor.

"We bagged a cruiser," O'Toole broke in. His jaw thrust out aggressively as he spoke. He intended to find somebody who was impressed by their victory.

Captain Midford nodded. "According to reports the Japs have hundreds more, and all of them headed this way." He looked at O'Toole a moment then pulled a blank toward him. "Weight? Class?"

"Ten thousand tons or more, I'd say. I don't know the class," Marty answered.

"She don't have much class now," O'Toole said and grinned widely.

"Any damage to your ship?"

"One wing will have to be doped and we need a new tail assembly," Marty answered. "No serious damage."

"Colonel Keller wants to see you boys." Midford smiled for the first time.

"What's funny?" O'Toole growled.

Captain Midford fixed the irate boll weevil with a cold look. "Say, sir, when you speak to a superior officer," he snapped

O'Toole batted his eyes and straightened up a little. "Yes, sir," he said.

Marty grinned as he turned away from the desk. O'Toole followed him out into the sunshine.

"A fine outfit, these flyin' marines," the Texan growled. "Here we come in after sinkin' a battlewagon, and what do we get?" He lifted his voice: "Say, 'Sir,' when you speak to a commanding officer!"

"The colonel may have a real job for us. He may be sending us to bomb Tokio," Marty said with a twinkle in his eyes.

"We wouldn't get any credit if we dropped one smack on the Mikado's front porch," O'Toole muttered.

They entered the office of Colonel Keller and

stood at attention while he finished signing a number of orders. When he had laid aside his pen he looked up.

"Excellent work, gentlemen," he greeted them. "I have had a radio report from the bombers who supported you. We'll show them what sea fighting really is."

O'Toole brightened up like a cat that has been stroked. Marty answered:

"Thank you, sir. We were to report to you for special duty."

"I have some work you boys can do." The colonel shuffled through his papers and flattened out a map. "How does that Sikorsky handle? Is she in good shape?"

"She is in good shape, sir. She is old and not very fast, but she can fly with any utility plane," Marty answered.

"You have flown her, Lieutenant, and can handle her better than anyone else I have. You will take over patrol duty. Lieutenant O'Toole and Sergeant Emory will be your crew. I have no other men to detail to you. Your work will be long range scouting. Sergeant Emory has been working with my Operations men and will be prepared to handle the radio reporting in code. You will be given instructions and routing when you report to patrol wing." He looked at Marty thoughtfully as he added: "This is a vitally important job. We are expecting an invasion."

"Yes, sir," Marty answered.

O'Toole's grin had faded, but he straightened a bit and saluted along with Marty. They walked out of the colonel's office and across the street to Wing Patrol.

"This is the dumbest war I ever fought in," O'Toole muttered. "Here we are, two of the best fighter pilots in the marine corps, and what do we get? We get insulted for sinking a cruiser, and the pay-off is patrol duty in an old crate built for hauling supplies."

"It's an important job," Marty reminded him.

"There won't be any excitement, just flittin' around over the China Sea," O'Toole grumbled.

"Listen to me, cotton-duster. There'll be

plenty of excitement the first time we bump that old betsy into a formation of Jap fighter planes. She's the best target the marine corps owns." Marty wasn't smiling when he said it. "If you ask me, this is a suicide job."

O'Toole brightened up at once. "Mebby they'll send us up to take a peek at the Jap coast."

"How about Formosa?" Marty asked. "The Japs will start their invasion from there. Formosa will be crawling with archies and fighter planes."

"Come on, let's get going," O'Toole said eagerly.

Patrol Wing was a big room with a large table in the center. Officers stood around the table looking at a great map of the China Sea area. There were army, navy and marine corps men in the group.

Marty reported to a marine colonel. The colonel turned them over to a dapper Philippine lieutenant.

"Lieutenant Cerez, these men are your patrol pilots," the colonel said.

Cerez nodded and smiled broadly. "You are?" He paused.

"Rivers and O'Toole," Marty said.

"Lieutenant Rivers, Lieutenant O'Toole, I am charmed." His eyes flicked over the Texan's sloppy uniform and his drooping figure. "I have your maps and routes laid out for you. When you have gone over the maps carefully you will check your flying boat and be ready for dawn patrol."

Marty and O'Toole found a vacant table and began studying their assignment. Their route was a wide circle with many side trips. Marty saw at once that they were to scout a large area of the China Sea. Their territory covered an area between the north coast of Luzon and the south end of the island of Formosa, a great spread of sea.

"Looks like a big chunk of the ocean," O'Toole said doubtfully.

"It shows just how short of patrol boats they are. We know that though, because they wouldn't be sending the Sikorsky out if they had enough PBY's," Marty pointed out.

"The upper edge of the course is within easy range of interceptors based on Formosa," O'Toole said with a wide grin.

"We'll run down and have a look at the Sikorsky." Marty gathered up the maps and orders.

They grabbed a car at the gate and rode down to the landing. Emory was waiting for them and scowling bleakly.

"What's up, Sergeant?" Marty asked.

"You should see the crew of mechanics they handed me, sir. I think they're all Japs," Emory answered.

"Are they good mechanics?" Marty asked with a grin.

"Yes, sir. They know what to do, but I don't like them."

"This your first trip to the Far East?" Marty asked.

"Yes, sir," Emory answered.

"I'll have a look at your crew," Marty answered.

Emory led the way to his shop. Marty looked at the six men detailed to Sergeant Emory. They were dark-skinned islanders, all of them undoubtedly citizens and hot blooded patriots. He walked over to them and talked with their corporal. The corporal grinned eagerly and proudly. He spoke precise English.

"Have any trouble with Jap spies?" Marty asked.

"Yes, sir, much trouble. They are everywhere." The corporal's smile widened. "But we fix them, sir. When we find a bad Phillipino or a Jap off he goes to jail."

"Do many of your people help the Japs?" Marty asked. "A few do, for large pay and bribes that are offered." His smile vanished. "They are no good. We find them but it is slower than with the Japs. We watch all of the time. Even in the shops we sometimes have them. But we watch."

"Good work, Corporal. "We don't want any-one fooling around our flying boat," Marty said.

"No," the corporal agreed. "I keep watch like the eagle."

"All your boys are good men?" Marty went on.

"Three I have had with me a long time. Two came today from shops in Manila. I will watch these new boys very careful." The corporal nodded toward his smiling helpers.

Marty turned away. He walked down to the float with O'Toole and Emory. He was satisfied the sergeant was unduly suspicious, yet he knew the Japs had been laying plans for a long time. They would be bound to have a few inside contacts in the mechanic groups.

The Sikorsky lay waiting for her crew. She was trimmed up as well as could be expected, considering her age and the natural wear and tear of many voyages. Marty went over her and found that Emory had her in first class shape. When he had finished his inspection he turned to Emory.

Either you or the corporal should be with the ship at all times. I believe the corporal can be trusted so that you can take your regular time off. He has been in service a long time and these boys are loyal. Just keep an eye open. I don't think anyone knows the old Sikorsky is going into actual service, but we'll take no chances.

O'Toole was waiting for them at the shop. "I'm hungry as a bear, let's hit for barracks," he said.

Marty grinned. "We're off," he said.

CHAPTER 7 DAWN PATROL

THE SUN was still below the horizon when Patrol Flight Seven manned the Sikorsky at Sangley Point base. The Sikorsky rested on the ramp. Hurriedly Marty checked engines, controls and motors. He could use only one small bulb for light but satisfied himself that the amphibian was ready.

Eerie, bluish wisps of flame played from the exhaust stacks. Marty bent forward impatiently. O'Toole had refused to hurry his breakfast and now they were late.

The beach men removed the beaching gear and Marty eased the throttle open enough to taxi to

117

the take-off area. There was more than enough
light to make buoys and other obstructions
visible. O'Toole jerked up his safety belt and
gave himself over to applying his toothpick. The
water lapped against the side of the hull as they
slid effortlessly into the harbor. Then came reports from the plane station.

"Beaching gear free, waist hatches closed,
ready for take-off. Radio ready for take-off."

Marty taxied out and weather-cocked into the
wind, then eased the throttle forward. Grad-
ually the propellers gnawed great chunks of air,
pulling the Sikorsky forward at increasing
speed. The engines burst into a roar like a thousand horses galloping over a bridge. Soon they
were up on the step, skipping along the water
as their speed increased.

As Marty lifted the Sikorsky up above clumps
of cottony cumulus clouds and leveled off, he
looked down. Below lay a generous portion of
the seven thousand islands comprising the Phil-
lipines. From ten thousand feet altitude each
island looked just like its outline on the chart.

Marty's brow furrowed. He was trying to remember something he had failed to do. He couldn't think what it was but he knew it was important. It worried him to have the thought lurking in the back of his mind and not to be able to remember what it was.

O'Toole was leaning back, taking life very easy. He was still picking his teeth but he looked as though he were about to drop off to sleep.

"Wake up! You're an observer and forward gunner!" Marty shouted.

O'Toole started and hunched forward. He peered down at the sea, then leaned back again.

"Nothing to observe," he grunted.

Suddenly Marty remembered what it was he had forgotten to do. He had intended to check ship himself before leaving. Being late he had not done it. He wondered if Emory had thought to go through lockers and compartments. He would ask the sergeant when he came forward. The Sikorsky was big and roomy and loaded light except for her gasoline storage. Suddenly

Marty grinned. He was certainly getting jittery, worrying about stowaways at a time like this.

They droned on, heading north and a few points west. The sea lanes they would cover were natural routes for troop transports heading south for landings at Aparri or Lingayen. Below them the sea was revealed by the rising sun. It shimmered deep blue and vacant—not a ship in sight. Marty checked his instruments and eased himself deeper against his shock pad.

O'Toole was dozing at his side but Marty did not rouse him. He could see everything there was to be seen below, which was exactly nothing. He felt a bit drowsy himself. Suddenly he felt a chill run down his spine. It started at the edge of his hair and trickled down like ice water. Before he could look around a guttural voice spoke.

"You are covered. Do not try to reach for a gun."

Marty twisted his head around. O'Toole lunged forward and jerked upright. Marty found himself looking into the muzzle of a submachine gun. A yellow face with a pair of slanting eyes regarded him coldly. Beside the little man stood another, just like him, and armed with another submachine gun, which was pointing at O'Toole's midsection.

"You-all be careful of them guns," O'Toole said softly. There was not the slightest trace of fear in his voice.

"What is this?" Marty demanded, though he knew well enough. He knew he had slipped up in not checking the ship. In some way the Japs had sneaked aboard and hidden.

The men were dressed in the garb of sugar laborers from the cane fields, but Marty knew they were soldiers, probably fliers. The man covering him spoke softly and his lips curled in a leer of triumph.

"We can fly this ship. If we must kill you we can fly it very well. I think you do not wish to be killed?"

Marty smiled grimly. "Certainly not," he said.

"Then you will obey orders. A man is back

in the radio room. He will operate the radio. You will deliver your ship to a port we tell you about." The precise English of the yellow man indicated he had been educated in an American school.

"Set the course," Marty said grimly. He had to have time to figure for a break. Three Japs armed with machine guns and willing to use them would be no push-over. On one point he had to be sure. He had to know whether the men were really fliers and navigators.

"You will hold your present course true. If you change it I will kill you and fly the plane myself," the Jap said. He grinned exposing a wide row of teeth.

Marty leaned back and began to ease off course very carefully, a few points only. He felt the muzzle of the Jap's gun jabbing into his neck.

"You will return to course," the man snarled.

Marty swung the Sikorsky back into line. The Jap knew navigation and was probably a flier, though he probably wasn't used to the bank of instruments on the Sikorsky. He glanced at his charts and at his compass. By holding their present line they would come in over Formosa.

O'Toole squirmed and leaned toward Marty. He spoke out of the side of his mouth. "I'm for chancing getting riddled. I don't aim to rot in no Jap jail, not with a war going on."

"Sit tight," Marty answered under his breath. "They'll kill us both if we start anything."

"Shut up, please!" The Jap guarding O'Toole spoke for the first time. His voice was high and squeaky.

The Sikorsky plowed ahead steadily. Marty looked down and nudged O'Toole. Far ahead he had sighted a big convoy. A line of warships plowed ahead of a mass of troop ships. This was the invasion force they had been sent out to locate. They would be unable to report its presence and it would proceed unmolested until it reached a point within range of light interceptors on patrol.

The Jap spies had cunningly learned which flying boat would patrol the lane of approach.

If he ever got out of the mess they were in Marty made up his mind he'd find out who had passed that information along to the enemy. Right now he could do no more than berate himself for not searching the ship before taking off.

The Jap seated behind him seemed to sense his thoughts. "The attack will be very much a surprise," he said with a wide smile. "It will be very successful. Within two weeks we will have overrun Luzon and destroyed the American fleet. For so boastful a race, you Americans are, as you would say, dumb."

O'Toole squirmed and his big hands balled into fists. He began muttering to himself.

"Be still, you!" the Japs snarled.

O'Toole lasped into silence. Marty watched the fleet below. He estimated the infantry force aboard those transports to be at least fifty thousand men. There were probably tanks and field guns and armored cars, too.

Sourly he regarded the vessels. A flight of Fortresses or divebombers could have wrecked the whole show. But the bombers would not get warning in time.

The convoys slipped behind them and Marty began looking ahead. There had been no chance at all to attack their captors. The Japs sat with their guns jammed up against the backs of the pilots, fingers curled around the triggers, slanting eyes fixed upon their victims, much as a cat watches a mouse it has trapped between its paws.

After a long period of smooth flying Marty saw land ahead. That should be the shoreline of Formosa. The Jap in command spoke softly.

"We do not wish to put you into prison. We will allow you to abandon ship. You may jump and use your parachutes."

Marty looked down at the choppy sea below. The shore was miles ahead. There would be no chance at all of a man reaching that shore once he landed in the sea.

"That is nice of you," he said in a steady voice. "When do we bail out?"

"Now," the Jap hissed. "I will take over the

controls. I have watched you carefully and will be able to handle the ship." He jabbed his gun into O'Toole's back. "You step back first."

As O'Toole rose he lurched against Marty and Marty whispered.

"I'm going to roll the old gal when you step between those two gunmen."

"Shoot," O'Toole hissed.

"Hands up! Get back quick!" the Jap snarled as he stepped aside to let the Texan pass.

O'Toole lurched backward and as he went Marty gave the controls a savage twist and gunned the motors. The Sikorsky came out of her placid, level flight with a slapping jerk. She doubled over and began spinning like a button on a string. Marty heard O'Toole's Texas rebel yell. A gun exploded close to his head, then something came crashing forward.

Marty righted the Sikorsky after pulling her out of the spin. The object which had hurtled forward was one of the Japs. The man started to rise, hunching forward with his chin sticking out, his eyes glaring madly. He was still clutching his machine gun, lifting its muzzle toward Marty's life belt. Marty's fist shot out and he clipped the Jap squarely on the chin. The little yellow man's knees buckled and his head snapped back. The machine gun clattered to the runway between the seats. Then the Jap sagged backward and collapsed.

"O'Toole!" Marty shouted. He hoped the boll weevil hadn't smashed his head against a girder and been knocked out. The flip he had done was bound to be rough on a loose man in the companionway.

"I got the monkey!" O'Toole shouted. "He bashed his head on a girder. But one got away!"

"I got him up here. Get a machine gun and go back to the radio!"

"Don't need any machine gun. I've got my 45!" O'Toole yelled. "I'm heading back!"

A moment later Marty heard the roar of the Colt and the staccato rattle of a machine gun. The machine gun stuttered and ceased firing, the 45 hammered away twice more. Marty grinned. He eased the inter-com telephone over to him.

"Hello, Texas."

"It's me, Emory," came a weak voice.

"Radio in a report on that convoy. Hurry."

"Yes, sir," came the weak voice of Emory.

"Are you badly hurt, Sergeant?" Marty asked.

"Just nicked. The lieutenant will help me." Emory answered. His voice faded to almost a whisper.

Marty waited as he swung around. He listened intently for the voice of Emory, calling in several times. The sergeant did not answer. Presently O'Toole's voice came over.

"That yellow rat got Emory in the arm. The kid jumped him when you turned her over. I've cleared a report to base." Marty heard O'Toole chuckle. "Reckon the surprise will be on the Jap fleet."

Looking into his rear view mirror Marty caught his breath. Six land-based fighters were closing in on the Sikorsky. He called back to O'Toole.

"Six fighters on our tail. Can you take the rear gun?"

"I'm warming her up this minute!" O'Toole called back. "Only yer crazy, there's twelve of them."

"Hang on, we're going to do some stunts," Marty ordered.

With only one gunner the big flying boat could not put up much of a scrap, but they could try. The Jap lying beside him stirred and Marty had to keep an eye on him. Suddenly the voice of Emory came in.

"I can man a gun, sir."

"Sure you're fit?"

"I'm fit," Emory answered. "My stomach has settled."

"Take the rear gun, Sergeant, and send Lieutenant O'Toole up here. Hold your fire until I give the order, no matter how close they get."

"Yes, sir," Emory answered.

A few minutes later O'Toole appeared. The Jap was sitting up, blinking his eyes and scowling. O'Toole had brought a length of cable with him. He jerked the prisoner to his feet and tied his hands behind him, then trussed his ankles.

"There, that'll hold you. If we're shot down

I'll loosen your hands and feet just to show you what a white man does even for a rat."

The Jap glared up at O'Toole. "You'll be shot down," he snarled. "You are flying back and that is a sign to attack."

"That's an idea," Marty said. He looked down at the Jap. "If we fly on to Formosa will they attack?"

"They will not," the Jap answered. "If you land and surrender they will not shoot you."

Marty grinned. "Thanks, pal," he said. "Suppose we take a little trip over their base. We might see something worth reporting."

"A good idea," O'Toole agreed. "But you better get squared around or we'll be drilled." He moved back. "I'll just man the upper cluster of guns. We might get a chance to use 'em."

Marty banked and circled while the fighter planes closed in. He dipped his wings as he passed under the formation and their leader returned the signal. Marty grinned broadly. The fighters circled and fell in behind and on each side. Four more had joined the escort, making sixteen in all. Marty built up altitude as he neared the mainland.

"Some procession," O'Toole called in. "The Mikado furnishes an escort for honorable amphibian." Marty heard him laugh softly.

"Better be thinking of a good maneuver. Those boys are tagging along to make sure we land," Marty answered.

"If we only had a rackful of bombs," O'Toole lamented. "We could sail right down and lay our eggs in their hair."

"And then what would happen?" Marty asked.

"Well, after that we'd flit homeward. I'm beginning to get hungry." O'Toole came forward and seated himself beside Marty. "I'll take over up ahead in a few minutes. I got a big idea." He craned his neck and looked at a fighter plane boring away just off their wingtip. "Not bad crates," he said and seemed to have forgotten his big idea.

Ahead loomed land. Marty could see a towering mountain peak far inland toward the center of the island. That would be Niitakiyama, rising fourteen thousand feet above the sea. He could also see the rugged outline of Mount Sylvia far to the north.

He remembered the advice of a gray-haired leatherneck who had once visited Formosa. The coastal area was like Japan but the hill country still belonged to the Taiyalas, who were the friends of no one.

Emory was calling from the rear gun. "A fighter is hanging close on our tail, sir." His voice sounded eager.

"Keep your guns off him until I give the word. How's the arm?" Marty called back.

"A bit stiff, sir, but I can operate this gun."

"I'll let you know what we plan to do," Marty promised. "We will not land unless we have to."

Up ahead the leader of the fighter squadron was dipping down, signalling for Marty to cut his altitude. Marty's grin widened.

"You said you had a plan?" he called to O'Toole.

The lead fighter dipped more urgently and two fighters zoomed down over the hatch cover of the Sikorsky threateningly. Marty noted that they carried light cannon as well as machine guns. He nosed the Sikorsky down and jiggled his wings.

"If we only had a full gun crew, what we'd do to those babies for shovin' us around that way! About the idea—I'll pop it in a minute."

"Look!" Marty shouted. "Up ahead!"

Far ahead, beyond rows of low buildings and blackened factory chimney stacks, they could see hangars and runways. The air base was a big one and located on low ground beyond a rolling line of hills. He wondered if theirs was not the first foreign plane ever to ride over the powerful base. Eagerly he took in all of the details so that later he could make a map.

There were two rail lines, a number of broad highways and then, over the low hills, the flying field. Marty judged it was fifteen miles inland and very well protected. A dozen big ships rode in the harbor. Out in deeper water lay a battleship and six cruisers. The place probably swarmed with speedboats.

"We can't land on that field out there,"

O'Toole growled. "Even a Jap ought to know that."

"No, but the fighters will have to land out there," Marty said.

"There! That's all my idea needed!" O'Toole shouted.

"Check the wind," Marty ordered.

"Cross wind. We'll have to come in between that battleship and the big cruiser," O'Toole answered.

"The yellow monkeys think they are perfectly safe," Marty said and chuckled.

"My idea is to prop our Jap up, untie his hands and make him give the idea he's landing this plane. Then the fighters may go on in and land," O'Toole said.

"A swell idea," Marty agreed.

"This fellow outside my port keeps craning his neck and so does the one on your side," O'Toole said. "I figure it will work."

"We'll go down over the harbor and kick up a little water. If the fighters go on in to their field we'll make a run for it and hope for the best," Marty said. He was checking the harbor below.

"Quite a fog of smoke coming from those factories," O'Toole observed. "If you edge over that way a bit it will help to fool them. They'll drop over the hill before we start up."

"Get that Jap up here," Marty said.

"Scoot over and lift the ship up a bit, like she'd hit a layer of air so as to shake off those nosy birds on the wings. I'll get the Jap into place." O'Toole's big mouth was twisted into a broad grin.

"Jab your Colt into his ribs and thumb the hammer back," Marty said as he slid over and took control from the seat of the co-pilot. He let the Sikorsky rise quickly and the fighter planes on either side disappeared.

The Jap seemed surprised when O'Toole freed his hands and shoved the gun into his ribs. O'Toole didn't have time to fool around. He picked up the Jap and plunked him into the pilot's seat, then crouched at his side.

"Now fly her in!" O'Toole bellowed. "Wave

at yer little pal when he bobs up again." He rammed the Colt threateningly against the ribs of the Jap.

Marty slid down into his seat so as to be out of sight. They were taking a long chance. He had the controls jammed with his foot to keep the Jap from diving the ship, but he wouldn't be abl᾿ to keep them that way long. The Jap might have a lot of suicide ideas.

The fighter pilots had appeared again, hugging the wing-tips. The pilot in the fighter plane looked across and nodded. Marty pulled his foot away and the Jap pilot dived the Sikorsky down. As they went Marty saw the fighter plane rise up and straighten out. He was probably telling the others that their man had taken over for a landing. Anyway that was what Marty was going to suppose he was doing.

"Drag him out of there!" he shouted. "He's about to turn us over."

The Sikorsky dived downward, then laid over on one wing, then dived again while Marty fought to take over. O'Toole ended the struggle by yanking the Jap out of the seat and flopping him on the narrow runway.

"Tie his hands and then man the forward cannon!" Marty shouted. "The fighters are going in and we're making a run for it."

The fighter planes, believing their man was flying the Sikorsky, were kiting away over the hill toward their field. Marty nosed the amphibian down and headed her for the smooth water which spread below. He had to go clear down in order to shake the fighter pilots. He wanted them to unload and leave their planes.

The bay and docks loomed close under their wings. Men appeared on the decks of the ships out in the bay. Marty scanned the scene. Apparently everyone had been warned that the ship was a captive. No guns barked at them. Marty scanned the scene. They had one break. The wind would make a low circle over the port necessary, and the nose of the Sikorsky would be headed out to sea.

"Chalk down everything you see as we go over the docks. Later we'll make a map," he called into the phone.

Two speedboats put out from the docks. They would get left far behind and need not be reckoned with. A third speedboat appeared, coming around from behind the battleship. It was armed with anti-aircraft cannon. Marty figured its probable speed and course and swung away from it. This laid his course almost into the shadow of the cruiser.

Gently the Sikorsky settled down over the water. Marty listened, tense, his muscles knotted. He felt the tops of the gentle swells tap at the hull and eased the motors open a little. The Sikorsky flitted along, skimming over the water, heading close under the bows of the cruiser. The speedboat had swerved and was cutting in on them. Marty saw that its guns were coming down to bear on the amphibian.

"Pot that speedboat!" Marty shouted to O'Toole. "Emory, stand by the rear gun. We'll have to rake their decks."

He gave the Sikorsky everything she had and headed her straight for the speeding boat so that O'Toole could get a good aim. O'Toole opened up savagely with the 50-calibre machine gun instead of the cannon.

A startled group on the deck of the onrushing boat ducked and scrambled for cover as the boll weevil's shells smashed the deck to splinters and ripped holes in her hull. The Sikorsky answered when Marty pulled her up. She raked over the deck of the boat and started to climb into the sky.

The cruiser came to life with a sudden burst of gunfire. The blast roared over their heads and burst in great puffs high in the sky. A bank of machine guns began drumming from the rear deck and bullets raked the Sikorsky from end to end.

Emory's tail gun opened up and the men on the deck of the cruiser dived and rolled for cover. As they bored up past the ship Marty laid back with all his strength, lifting the Sikorsky as fast as she would take it. She responded

nobly and lifted into the blue at a rapid pace—
Marty wanted to shout! The old girl still had
what makes the aircraft of the U.S.A. first in
the world's heavy planes.

And now the whole harbor had come to life.
Guns on shore hammered away, their shells
screaming wildly up in long arcs. Tracer bullets marked the sky into a crisscross pattern
while the old amphibian showed her heels to the
whole might of the Mikado's naval forces.

Marty did not try for altitude after he had
got a few thousand feet under his wings. He
opened the radials wide and ran for it. The
more distance he put between them and the
mainland before the interceptors took off again,
the better would be their chances of escape.

The air speed showed two hundred and fifty
and that was far beyond the rated speed of the
Sikorsky. Marty checked his compass and instruments. He laid over and headed a few
points west. Now the turn and bank indicator
was centered, the gyro compass and the gyro

horizon gave him the ship's position. Marty settled back and let the giant vibrate, hoping both her motors would stay in their mountings.

"Sight anything on our tail?" he called back to Emory.

"Fighters coming up," Emory called back.

Marty made some rapid calculations. The fighters would be at least a hundred miles per hour faster than the Sikorsky. Roughly he figured that for every mile he would make they would cover one and three quarters. The chase promised to be a hot one, as the interceptors had a probable range of around four hundred miles.

After hammering along for a while he called back to Emory again. "How are we doing, Sergeant?"

"They are closing in, sir. There are twelve of them." Emory sounded cheerful. Just a bit eager to have the Japs get within gun range.

"I'm not hanging around to fight them," Marty said. "What we need is a fog bank or a blackout."

O'Toole's drawl came in. "Cloud bank off the port wing, Mister Rivers. If you-all feel like running upstairs and hiding."

"I'm running!" Marty called back.

The Sikorsky nosed upward and quartered toward a distant line of white clouds. Marty looked back and estimated their chances of escape. He guessed them to be about fifty-fifty.

As the Sikorsky hit the climb her speed dropped to two hundred, then to one eighty and finally hung at one sixty. The fighters came on, darting like dragon flies. Marty was aware one of them had closed in when he heard Emory's gun open up. The cloud layer was still above and ahead of them.

He caught a flash of a twisting, flaming ship as it dived past. Emory had potted the first one and it was going down in a spin, burning as it twisted toward the sea. O'Toole was scrambling to the gun in the midsection. He didn't aim to miss out on any shooting. Marty heard him open up.

The fate of the first fighter to close in caused the others to zoom upward and bank for position above the flying boat. In that brief space Marty got the Sikorsky up above the cloud layer and dived her for cover. Stringers of mist reached out like arms trying to pull them into a giant feather bed. The Sikorsky buried her nose in the mist and then vanished into gray gloom.

Marty had never liked flying in a cloud or dense fog. It always gave him the jitters. But this thick, damp blanket had a friendly feeling, a warm cosiness that made him laugh outright.

"What you-all cacklin' about?" O'Toole barked over the phone. "You sneaked out without letting me get a decent shot."

"You won't get a shot if this cloud layer holds out," Marty called back.

The clouds held out and the Sikorsky hammered along. Marty eased her down to cruising speed and let her drill along. He checked his compass and plotted his course. When he felt sure they were clear of the interceptors he straightened her and headed for home. Then he called to Emory.

"See what you can do about making a chart of that port."

He got no answer so he called O'Toole. "See what happened to Emory."

"Going back," O'Toole answered promptly.

A full five minutes later O'Toole's voice came through. "The kid's passed out cold. He got a lot worse package than I thought. He had pulled his jacket over the wound to keep me from seeing it." For once O'Toole's voice was troubled. "Step her up a bit. We have to get the kid to a saw-bones."

Marty shifted course. Making a direct run meant leaving the nearby bank of clouds, but it had to be done if time was to be saved.

CHAPTER *8* WILDCATS WITH WINGS

MARTY BROUGHT the Sikorsky down on the smooth waters of Manila Bay. As he taxied in a naval crew swarmed out to take over. O'Toole had Emory ready to transfer to an ambulance. Marty stayed to hand over the prisoners.

"Report in for me," O'Toole called. "I'm going with the kid."

A marine sergeant and four men took over the prisoners, while the navy boys, headed by an ensign, took over the Sikorsky. The officer snapped a salute, then smiled up at Marty who was prodding his prisoners out of the hull door.

"If you two leathernecks keep on you'll be getting a reputation for being lucky, sir," he said.

"I'll be lucky if I save my stripes this time," Marty answered. Then he added, "You better do some checking among the men on beach work. I have a hunch someone has been passing along aid and comfort to the enemy."

"We've been at it already," the officer answered.

Before reporting in, Marty made several rough maps of the base area he had flown over and the Jap defenses at Tainan. He wanted to jot down all he remembered before any of it slipped out of his mind.

Captain Midford looked up as he entered. The captain smiled broadly. "Nice work, Rivers. It gives me the jumping jitters to sit here pushing a pencil while you fellows have all the fun."

Marty reached for a pad and began filling out his report. He signed one for O'Toole while he was at it.

"We had a bit of action today," he admitted as he shoved the report across the desk.

Then he headed for Colonel Keller's office before the commander had a chance to send for him. The colonel looked up from his desk as an orderly ushered Marty in. He nodded toward a chair.

"I was expecting you," he said dryly.

"I thought it best to report at once, sir," Marty said as he laid his maps on the desk.

The colonel pulled them over to him and scanned each one carefully. He made several notes on one of them, then looked up.

Marty was putting a lot of hope on those maps, depending on them to square him. He had not checked his ship before taking off and had almost lost the amphibian, that was serious.

"These are remarkably well done," the colonel said as he tapped one of the maps with his pencil. "In fact they are almost as accurate as the maps our intelligence department has prepared for us." A thin smile formed on his lips and there was a twinkle in his cold, blue eyes.

Marty felt a chill go down his spine. "I wish to report also, sir, that I took off without making a thorough search of ship. Three armed spies had come aboard." Marty plunged right into the trouble ahead of him.

The colonel picked up one of the maps. "I will amend my statement a little. This map shows valuable targets we had no knowledge of. It also gives us the location of certain units of the enemy fleet, which is valuable information."

Marty felt better. He grinned at the colonel.

"We have pieced together a very good picture of what happened to you. We picked up the enemy broadcast from your ship. We have located the man who passed on the information and the men who handled the work at the beach. Ordinarily this would reflect upon your record, but as that record can stand quite a lot of adverse matter and still be above the average, I am not going to mark down anything against you." The colonel's grim frown melted into a wide smile. "You did the marines proud, son, that's what I'm saying." He held out a hand.

Marty gripped the colonel's hand. He felt like shouting; instead he said:

"Thank you, sir."

"I have two Grumman fighter planes which the boys have patched up. I can assign them to you and to your Texas friend, Lieutenant O'Toole, if you still feel lucky."

Marty jumped to his feet. "Thank you, sir," was all he could say.

"Convey my compliments to Lieutenant O'Toole," the colonel said.

"I will, sir, and I know he will be tickled."

The colonel regarded him thoughtfully. "MacArthur is short of fighter planes and he is short of fliers. He seems to be short of many supplies he needs to meet an invasion. We are turning over the fighters we have, but you should know that your chances of staying in the air over Luzon are not good." He lifted a hand to his chin and frowned.

"Our equipment is superior, sir. The old Sikorsky showed her heels to a flight of their bombers," Marty said eagerly.

"We will have to take off the flying boats and the bombers because we will not have bases for them, and that will take men away from the general." He looked grimly at Marty. "What damage you do will be of great service, but eventually you will be wiped out. Is that clear?"

"Yes, sir. But an invasion won't get far," Marty leaned forward eagerly.

"With the spirit our forces are showing, this invasion will cost the enemy more than he can afford to lose in men and in valuable time. You fellows make me want to go up myself." The colonel saluted smartly. "Now get out!"

Marty rushed out of the office, almost upsetting an orderly who was entering with a pile of papers. He dashed for the barracks. O'Toole was seated at a table with four other fliers. The boll weevil had a steak, fried onions with a piled-up dish of corn bread on the side. This array was flanked by four glasses of buttermilk.

"Sit up and have a snack," he greeted Marty.

Marty grinned widely as he seated himself. Bill Chester was sitting across the table. The boys had been shooting questions at O'Toole without much success in getting information.

"Texas, here, tells us you landed in Tainan Bay, shook hands with an admiral, and then took off again." Bill laughed as he said it. "Just what did happen?"

"Yer not makin' me out a liar?" O'Toole gave Bill a reproachful look as he lifted a fresh glass of buttermilk.

"We just dropped in for tea and rice," Marty said.

The boys laughed. O'Toole went on eating. Marty turned to him. "The Old Man says we get two Grummans tomorrow and join the boys up north."

O'Toole had a large cut of steak almost in his mouth. He lowered his fork and straightened his hunched shoulders.

"Now they're doin' something to win this war," he drawled.

"You birds are plain lucky," Bill said. "We are marked down to ferry bombers and flying boats south."

"You'll like the Dutch," Marty said. "I flew down there on instruction once. They'll make you bat the corners off a lot of clouds to keep up with them."

"But the fighting is going on up here," Bill growled.

"According to the colonel it's apt to move south," Marty said.

"There'll be planes coming in from home," one of the boys said. "I don't see why we aren't left here."

"According to the colonel we'll fight it out with what we have," Marty said.

"But we can't do that. They'll be swarming over the islands like bees within a few days. I heard they were landing at Aparri right now. That will give them air bases," Bill argued.

"If what we saw is anything to go by they'll be landing at Lingayen, too," Marty said grimly. "How many divebombers went out after that convoy?"

"A dozen from our base. But they ran into fighter planes as thick as flies. I don't know whether many of them got through. I tried to wangle a seat in one of them but the older heads got the breaks."

O'Toole put down his fork and scowled at the portion of his steak still on his plate. "You birds plumb take away my appetite. Just you wait until tomorrow. I'm starting in at dawn to whittle me a lot of notches on the butt of me Colt."

"Right ho!" somebody said. "It's thumbs up!"

O'Toole shoved back his chair and yawned. "I'm tuckered out and need a bit of a nap," he said. Then he turned on his heel and sauntered away.

Bill Chester grinned as he watched the lank Texan amble away. "He's my idea of what the Texas Rangers are like. I'd hate to cross fire with him in the air."

"He's the craziest flier you ever saw," Marty agreed. "And one of the best to have in the slot next to you."

He got to his feet and went outside for a walk.

A warm wind carried the sounds and the smells of the city of Manila to him. He wondered, as he moved along a darkened street, when the first air blasting would come. Much depended upon the few fighter planes which would have to fend off an attack. After walking a few blocks he turned about and returned to barracks.

The next morning eleven fighters, two Wildcats and nine P–40's stood in line, their exhausts flaring under idling throttles. This was the dawn patrol and Marty and O'Toole were a part of it. They stood beside the flight officer and waited.

A youngster in an army outfit came up and saluted. He looked little over eighteen. His cheeks were soft and rosy and his eyes were eager. He wore the bars of a captain.

"I am Captain Dykes, gentlemen," he said in a voice that added to his appearance of youth.

Marty and O'Toole saluted. Dykes was their flight leader.

"I am told you marines are tough fighters," he said. "We're glad to have you with us. The going ought to get rough about sunup."

"That's what we like," Marty said. O'Toole just stretched his long neck and cast a disdainful eye upon the P–40's.

"We make a swing north and keep an eye open for bandits," Dykes said. "If any enemy planes are sighted you are to stay in formation and wait for orders." He seemed to feel he must put special emphasis on this point. Marty grinned at him.

"Yes, sir," Marty answered. O'Toole just grunted.

"Much depends upon this. We are very shorthanded in this man's war. The plans laid down are to be followed." Dykes saluted and turned away.

"The army's been robbin' cradles," O'Toole growled.

"Dykes is twenty-two," the ground officer said stiffly.

A few minutes later they climbed into their cockpits and slid their hatch covers forward. Marty tightened his life belt and eased himself back against the shock pad. It was good to be back in a Grumman Wildcat again, to have the feel of power and compactness and to know that eight wing guns poked out up ahead. He slid his thumb over the gun button eagerly.

"Flight Seven, are you ready?"

That was the voice of Dykes and over the radio it sounded like the high pitched voice of a school boy.

The pilots all cleared, O'Toole's drawl coming in last.

"Check your temperatures," Dykes ordered.

Marty caught the flash of the ground officer's shaded light and gunned the Wildcat, ramming down on one break. The Grumman came to life and snapped around. With a blast of prop pressure he hoiked her tail and sent her down the runway with the others. As he roared into the coming dawn a P-40 knifed over his hatch cover and went on up. Marty had a glimpse of Dykes bending forward in the yellow light of his instrument board. The kid was a bit reckless himself.

Marty dropped into position with O'Toole on his right and Dykes on his left. The captain had taken the two marines under his wing, possibly to make sure they didn't go off duck hunting. The others were coming up in formation, with the odd two making a formation off to the right.

"Up to three thousand." Dykes' high voice sounded thinner.

They went up with their flaming breath matching the red flush of the dawn. A solitary searchlight beam cut across the dome of night like a blade of a giant's sword. Back and forth it poked and slashed, then snapped off.

Marty gave his attention to his ship and his guns. He was all set for anything and hoping it would happen.

"Up to ten thousand," Dykes called.

Up went the fighters, their powerful engines roaring. The radial of the Grumman sounded sweeter to Marty than the drone of the Allisons in the P–40 ships, but he guessed the P–40's would be able to hold up their end.

Dawn soon lighted the island of Luzon and the sky above it. Flight Seven had been boring away without any talk between pilots for some time. Suddenly Operations back at their base began calling.

"Flight Seven! Flight Seven! Do you hear me? Come in, Flight Seven."

"Flight Seven reporting. We hear you clear and loud," Dykes called back.

"Bombers reported by Clark Field. Twenty-eight bombers supported by fighter craft. Flight Four going up from Clark Field. Flight Seven stand by to intercept." The headset rattled and the rest of the message blurred.

"Flight Seven standing by," Dykes called back.

"Whoopee!" came a shout from O'Toole, and Marty caught a snatch of the Texan's coon hunting song.

"Hold formation. Take fifteen thousand," Dykes piped. "Hold formation, Texas!"

Up went the mottled fighters, standing on their tails and reaching for the blue above. At fifteen thousand they leveled off and drove north through a cold layer of upper air. Dykes was letting his P–40 out, and Marty wondered if he thought he could show up the Grummans. He grinned and eased his Wildcat up ahead of the leader.

"Formation!" Dykes snapped.

"Mebby you-all better get out and push that crate," O'Toole drawled.

Marty heard a grunt from Dykes and then a chuckle. They were circling now, spinning a great web in the sky. Dykes came in and his voice cracked from high to low.

"Bandits below! Peel off and go down!"

Marty looked down and spotted the formation of bombers. Flight Four must have missed them. They were moving along in perfect formation. Then he looked to the north and saw what was delaying Flight Four. The sky was marked by great circles and spirals of exhaust smoke. Flight Four was in a savage dogfight with the interceptors of the bomber squadron. By all indications they were badly outnumbered.

There was no time to consider rushing to the

aid of Four. His turn had come to peel off and go down the glory trail. O'Toole had already gone screaming down the chute.

Marty laid over and went down with his motor playing a smooth tune, the blunt nose of the Wildcat breaking the crazy dive. A P–40 drilled past him, and then another. Those sharp-snouted babies could certainly dive. Marty held on and did not power his way down. He had his eye on two bombers that had broken away from their formation after a P–40 had slashed into it.

He selected the larger of the two bombers and went down on it. The bomber seemed huge and lumbering as it came into his sight. He depressed the gun button and his eight Brownings drilled their hail of bullets into the Mitsubishi.

It flamed once, wriggled in agony and belched a cloud of scarlet fire and dense smoke. With an up-twist it threw away its right motor, and a section of wing floated down toward the wooded country below.

Marty had a glimpse of bodies spilling out of

the flaming hull as he zoomed up under the other
bomber. He raked it and watched it sag away
with one wing bent upward. Then he went on
up and leveled off. From the top of his perch
he saw that Flight Seven was wrecking the
bomber formation. The bandits had scattered
and were diving away in every direction with
P–40's on their tails. Three were spiraling
downward in sluggish but certain descent. The
boys were doing themselves proud. Marty
spotted O'Toole's Wildcat far over to the right.
It was whirling and ducking around a bomber.

His Grumman began to settle and Marty sent
her roaring down after a bomber which had
ducked his way. Now the Jap pilots seemed to
have got some sort of order. They were all
ducking it toward the distant sky battle where
they might find protection from their own
fighter craft.

Flushed with victory Flight Seven began to
converge. "Flight Seven come in, close formation," Dykes was calling.

At that moment Marty glanced into his mirror and instantly shoved his controls over. A Karigane was spitting on his tail, raking the Grumman with lead. The Grumman went over and down with a neck-jerking dive. Marty let her roll over and come up under full throttle.

He shook the Karigane but no sooner was he leveled off than he found another Jap on his tail. The air was full of them. Marty grinned and cut his engine. The sharp-snouted Jap plane seemed oddly familiar to him. Suddenly he realized that it was a German Messerschmitt 109. His big radial motor served as a brake but the Me had no such brake.

Raging over Marty's hatch cover the Jap raked off the upper part of the bird cage. As he fired into the windscreen Marty let him have it with his eight guns. The tail assembly of the Me lifted and hurtled backward, sawed off as neatly as though cut by a knife. Marty went down just in time to escape the whirling wreckage.

The terrible power of those Brownings sent a chill up Marty's spine. He had no time to enjoy chills, however. Two more Karigane's had closed in and were peppering away, one coming up from below, the other coming down in what seemed to be an attempt to ram his Grumman.

"Flight Seven come in! Flight Seven come in! Do you hear me, Flight Seven?" That was the voice of Dykes and it sounded thin and strained.

As Marty laid the Grumman on her edge and knifed out of the tight spot he was in he spotted Dykes' P–40. The plane was wobbling and settling far below. Smoke was belching out of the cowling.

Marty went around in a screaming circle and headed down.

"Jump, Dykes, jump!" Marty shouted before he thought.

"Guess I'll take her in." The voice of Dykes was little more than a whisper.

Marty raged into his flap-mike but he got no answer. Diving down he shook off all of the Japs except one who was flying another of the ships looking like an Me. Marty wanted to get close enough to cover Dykes when he took to his silk. But the Me was too hot on his trail to allow him to keep on going down.

He laid over and went up again. As he went he saw that Dykes' P–40 was enveloped in a mass of flames. Dykes hadn't bailed out. A cold fear clutched at Marty's heart. Dykes was hit hard, no doubt about that. Then he saw the P–40 nosed into the jungle. It rolled and bounced like a ball of fire.

Marty saw no more because the Me was closing in again. He tried the trick he had used before—cutting his motor. The Me raged over his hatch cover and Marty cut loose. The Me dived and he missed clean. He saw that Flight Seven was forming for a return to base, but he couldn't obey orders with the Me on his hands.

Over he went, so close to the Jap plane that he could see its pilot. He had a start when a smiling face looked across at him for a split second. The pilot was no Jap, he was a white man, and his grin was broad.

"O.K., Jerry," Marty said softly. "Before I

get through with you, you'll think the **R.A.F.** is on your tail."

He swung off on one wing and spun the Grumman around, then dived her under full throttle. Coming up he made a tight loop across the path of the Me. He crossed the trail of the Me with his guns blazing. The maneuver was clearly a new trick for the Me's pilot.

Marty went down and as he went he looked into his mirror. The amazing Me was dipping its wings mockingly at him but it wasn't diving. It slid off on one wing and began sloping toward the north. Marty let it go and bored after his flight.

Five **P–40's** and two Grumman Wildcats rolled up to the line at the temporary air base. Marty wrenched loose what was left of his hatch cover and climbed out. O'Toole was waddling toward the briefing room. He halted and waited for Marty.

"Some show!" Marty said.

"Sure was," O'Toole agreed. "There must have been fifty of those yellow bats after us."

"They got Dykes."

"And two other boys. I saw one bail out." O'Toole halted just outside the door. "We got to have a few more planes," he said. It was the first time Marty had ever heard the Texan admit any sort of odds meant anything to him.

"Didn't I hear you say something about notches on your gun?" he asked.

"Yeah, and I'll get 'em, too, but they have to keep us supplied with crates. Mine got a package right back of the seat that about sawed her in two." He clamped his mouth tight shut, then added, "Same way Dykes' ship got it, only his took the load in front of the seat where Dykes was."

"I lost a hatch cover but I can fly without that," Marty said. "Goggles and a windscreen is all any man needs." He did not mention Dykes. Not that he would forget.

"Me, I'm worrying about being on foot," O'Toole said mournfully.

"We can always join MacArthur's tank outfit," Marty said.

"That's just where I'll be if they leave me sit on the ground," O'Toole answered.

There was silence and plenty of it in the briefing room. Flight Seven had been whittled down again and there were no replacements. The recording officer shoved report blanks across to them.

"Just to keep the record straight," he said.

"How's the invasion coming?" one of the men asked.

"Japs are landing in swarms at Lingayen and at Batangas."

Marty and O'Toole turned toward their barracks. O'Toole sniffed eagerly as they entered the lounge and coffee room. Marty beat him to it.

"I think I'll just have a snack to eat," he said.

"You took the words right out of my mouth," O'Toole said and grinned broadly. "I had to hurry through my breakfast. You kept yellin' at me to shake a leg."

Marty smiled. The boll weevel was normal again.

CHAPTER 9 WASHED OUT

FLIGHT SEVEN presented a sorry sight on the morning of December 26th. Two patched and riddled P–40's and one Grumman Wildcat was all that remained of the command. Grim-faced men worked around the three planes in desperate effort to make the craft fly. All the pilots of those three scarred ships asked of the ground crew was that they patch the fighters up so they would fly.

Marty Rivers' Wildcat was almost a different plane from the one in which he had started the Battle of Manila. It was an assembly of parts and pieces dug up by resourceful mechanics.

168

For many days the men had known that no machines or parts would get through to them. This was a flight to the bitter end, and that end would be a washout for every plane. It was just a matter of staving off the hour when the last pilot aloft would call in to Operations, "WASHED OUT!"

Marty stood watching the men as they loaded his Brownings. His face was lined with grim weariness. Flying sixteen hours a day with night defense thrown in had left its mark there, but not on his iron nerves. His hand was steady as he lifted it and glanced at his wrist watch.

O'Toole was out with him. The Texan had hoped the boys would be able to patch up his Grumman by replacing part of one wing with a section from a P-40. Emory was back on the job and doing wonders. But O'Toole would have to hurry if he was to join the flight going out.

Captain Midford was on the field. He no longer needed to stay in his office. The days of red tape and piles of reports were over. There was no longer any place to send the reports except to his files. The Japs had upset his years of routine.

With most of the air force gone to the Dutch bases where they would take over new planes coming from the United States, the Manila air units were mere skeleton crews.

There was no need for more men, nor could they be spared to be trapped on Luzon. Every pilot and every mechanic was valuable in the long pull that lay ahead. With Nichols and Clark fields blasted and useless the bombers had drifted south. Even the old Sikorsky had taken off with a load of airmen. Colonel Keller had gone out on the amphibian.

Marty grinned as he remembered the sulphurous words of the colonel when he received orders to shift his base of operations. The veteran devil dog had jumped up and down and pounded his desk, so the orderlies said. But he was a marine, and orders meant immediate action with him. He had rifled his files and left.

The Japs were swarming into Luzon from

both the north and the south. From Linguayen
two spearheads thrust south, driving down a
long valley, while another thrust was pushing
inland along the road from Aparri. This thrust
had separated at Tuguegarao. A force was
coming down from Vigan to the north also.
The southern armies were coming up from Mau-
ban and Atimonan. Yellow men swarmed everywhere. The general's troups, outnumbered
ten to one, were falling back step by step.

The Japs came trotting into the muzzles of
155-millimeter canon, or pedaled along roads on
bicycles with light machine guns on their backs.
Tough old campaigners and Philippino youths
charged the yellow horde with cold steel to close
the gaps made by Jap divebombers and tanks,
but the little yellow men swarmed in like war-
rior ants on the march.

As Marty stood waiting, much of this went
through his mind. In moments of idleness he
thought of such things, though generally the
desperate fighting at hand blotted out everything except his own job. Now he heard above

the rumble of the three idling motors the distant roar of incoming bombers. Moving forward impatiently he tapped a grimy corporal on the shoulder. The corporal straightened and saluted.

"Got her about ready?"

The corporal squinted up into the hot sky, located the flight of bombers, then turned back to Marty.

"She'll take off, sir, and she'll fly. But she's not safe for a dive or a roll that will put stress on this tail assembly. I spliced it in a few places, but we have no sections to put in."

"If she'll take off, clear her and stand by," Marty snapped.

The corporal stepped back and bellowed an order. He grinned at Marty and lifted a greasy hand.

"Happy landing, sir!" he said.

The other men stood aside as Marty climbed up. There was a light of admiration in their eyes. The mechanics and the butterfly men had come to think a lot of this big marine who flew any kind of a crate with the savage abandon of a test pilot putting a brand new ship through her paces.

Marty did not have to palm his hatch cover forward. He no longer had a hatch cover. He adjusted his goggles and flap-mike, then lifted a hand. Thumbs up!

Midford waved to him nervously. The men watched to see if the Grumman would make it off the ground. The radial motor roared and blasted her tail up. Down the field she went, pinched around and came back. The men stood watching, not a muscle moving in the whole group. When Marty hopped her off the ground a sigh of relief went up.

The Wildcat responded but not in the peppery, spirited way she had once acted. She was like an old race horse, still filled with fire but stiff in the joints and a bit slow.

Twelve bandits were coming in for a whack at Manila's water front. They were flying insolently, wing to wing in close formation. Marty squinted at them. They would have been easy targets for the old Flight Seven, even with the swarm of fighter support that swept along high above them, needling back and forth, watching and waiting for three crippled interceptors with red, white and blue markings on their rudders.

Below him Marty saw the two P–40's lift and swing upward. Three against thirty or forty. Nice odds, too bad O'Toole was grounded, Marty thought, and grinned to himself. He pictured the boll weevil down in the shop sweating and roaring as he tried to fix up a wing for his Grumman.

Making a wide circle he built up altitude. He had two reasons for not knifing straight up. First he might escape notice by the nearsighted fliers high above; second he might be able to get the drop on the fine parade the killers were staging and scatter them before they could do any bombing.

One thing Marty meant to do. He would fly the Grumman the same as though she were decked out in inspection tags, certifying her to be in perfect flight trim.

He got his altitude and came back, high above even the fighter escort. With a dip of his wings he sent the Grumman roaring down the chute. She wobbled a bit as she gained speed, and shuddered in every joint. Her dural surfaces seemed to be complaining of the strain, and her tail assembly quivered with every blast. Marty set his eyes on his sights and thumbed his gun button. He forgot all about the fighter planes. They would come screaming down after him, but he meant to get to the neat formation of bandits first.

The lead bomber came into his sight, lifted, grew bigger and clearer. They did not know he was dropping out of the sun to hammer them. His hand closed on his gun button. Grimly he watched his lead saw a ragged line across the bomber amidships. It buckled and instantly burst into flames. The formation broke as each killer whirled to flee. Marty pulled up and started his climb.

The Grumman answered this supreme test as best she could. But the best she could do was to

wiggle her way upward in a crazy manner. The
patched tail assembly had pulled out of line under
the strain of the dive. Operations began calling
in an anxious voice.

"Flight Seven! Flight Seven! Can you hear
me?"

"Rivers of Flight Seven. I can hear you loud
and clear," Marty called back. "One bandit
down. Am returning to the attack."

The two P–40's reported in and that made
Marty feel better. "One Jap down. One Jap
on fire."

The boys were getting in their work. Marty
saw that no planned bombing of the port would
be carried out by this group. They were scatter-
ing and unloading as fast as they could without
trying for a target.

The Grumman was still fighting for altitude
from which to drive down upon another of the
bombers when a swirling attack struck her. Four
blunt-nosed, low-winged Kariganes converged on
her savagely. Their bullets sprayed over the

Grumman and splattered around Marty. Out
of the corner of his eye Marty saw that the P–40's
were in the same tight spot.

Flattening the Wildcat, Marty stood her on
her nose. She would have to make one more dive
or be riddled. As he came over he got a Jap in
his windscreen and let him have it. The Jap
kited up into the blue, then fell off in a tight spin.

Lead was again pelting the wings, and fuselage
and motor of the Grumman. Marty kept her
diving. It was his only hope. She wrenched and
twisted as she went down, then she began to spin.

Fighting desperately he managed to pull her
out of the spin, but before he had flattened out he
saw two Kariganes knifing down for the kill.
Marty did what he should have done and tried to
bring the Grumman up and out of their line of
fire. She lifted sluggishly, but enough to clear
their savage thrust.

Marty cuddled his flap-mike. In about a minute he'd be checking out. The Grumman wasn't
responding to her rudder. The two fighters were

making a tight circle, coming in on his tail. Their snouts were blurred by spurts of flame from their hub cannons.

The shells smashed into the Grumman and exploded. Her motor coughed wearily, backfired twice, then went dead. Marty put her into a dive. He had to go down fast, even if she didn't hold together. The Japs circled and came down in power dives.

Suddenly Marty jerked forward and craned his neck. He bit off the words he had started to call in to Operations. A fighter plane with the stars of the U.S.A. on her wings was cutting down on the tails of the two Kariganes. The plane was a Grumman Wildcat with a funny looking right wing. Mike O'Toole was coming down the chute like a wild man!

Marty whooped and eased over a little, to see better rather than to escape from the Japs. The Japs did not sight O'Toole until he had them in a tight spot. By the time they roared over Marty's unprotected head they were in headlong flight with lead spraying them and raking their cockpits. Behind them came O'Toole like an avenging knight. One Karigane burst into flames. The other ducked but guessed wrong. He ducked the same way that O'Toole banked and his right wing folded back like a barn door in a tornado.

"You-all better hike in," O'Toole drawled. In spite of his drawl Marty knew the Texan was worried. "I'm king of the air up here and I'll clean up the strays."

"Go to it!"

"Whoopee!" O'Toole shouted. He was so glad Marty was alive and not a riddled corpse that he flung his Grumman over on its back and did a roll.

Marty gave his attention to getting the Grumman in. She wanted to roll over and go down on her back and nose. He fought her all the way in and set her down with a bounce that sounded like dumping a sack of scrap pots into a bin. She slewed around, skidded and went in on one wheel.

Men rushed forward. Two of them had a

stretcher. One carried a fire extinguisher. They swarmed up on the Grumman but Marty waved them aside.

"I'm not even touched," he said, grinning, as he jumped down.

The men looked open-mouthed from the riddled Grumman to her pilot. Sergeant Emory laughed suddenly.

"Lady Luck, sir," he shouted.

Marty turned to the ship. There was hardly a part of the Wildcat which had not been punctured. Gas dripped from her tanks and made a pool under her. She had a gaping hole in her right wing and half of her motor assembly, including her prop, had been blasted away. Marty grinned.

"It didn't seem that hot up there," he said.

Then he saw that the P–40's had not come in. He looked up into the sky. A lone fighter was circling, and diving, and slashing in and out of a Jap formation. That was O'Toole.

Marty turned to Emory.

"We lost both of the Curtiss ships, sir. But we

got three bombers and six interceptors," Emory said.

Marty wiped a sweat-soaked hand across his forehead, then grinned at the silent men around him. "Shouldn't wonder if you'd have to raise that count three or four more. O'Toole is still upstairs."

The men laughed and that broke the tension. Every eye was turned upward and they stood watching the Texas boll weevil put on a show. It lasted only a few minutes longer. O'Toole ran out of ammunition and then showed the Japs a few things about stunting.

The cotton-duster played tag with death so long Marty began to scowl. Finally, with a disdainful dive through the center of the Jap formation, O'Toole came in. The boys on the ground guns scrambled to cover his landing. But the Japs did not want any lead from the ground.

O'Toole came roaring in low over Marty's head. He bounced his wheels off the roof of the machine shop, banked with one wing a few feet off the turn, then rolled in and up to the shop.

Marty grinned as the lank Texan climbed out of his ship. O'Toole stood looking at Marty's ship.

"Where was you-all sittin'?" he asked.

"In the lap of Lady Luck," Marty answered.

"A fine gal," O'Toole said.

"Looks like you were Flight Seven until I can get a lot of court plaster pasted on my Wildcat and a tail assembly installed," Marty said.

"Yeah," O'Toole answered and his mouth curled into a scowl. "Miller bailed out when he got on fire. Three yaller rats gunned him on the way down." O'Toole jerked off his helmet. "I checked the crazy stuff painted on the sides of their crates. I'll know 'em when we meet again." His eyes glinted like broken glass.

Marty did not have to ask what would happen to those three Japs. He turned toward the ground crew.

"Patch her up, fellows," he said. "Try to have her ready by tomorrow morning."

"Yes, sir," Emory answered.

"I'm staying in the air until we go over Tokio,

and no yaller Jap is going to knock me off," O'Toole said.

Marty did not argue. No use in suggesting that they might have to stay on Luzon. If the island fell they'd fall with it and go into a stockade along with what would be left of the general's tough fighters. O'Toole seemed to catch what Marty was thinking.

"They may corner the general, but I figure he'll never run up the white flag." O'Toole shrugged his shoulders as he turned toward the briefing room.

"Right you are," Marty agreed, and felt mean for even thinking of defeat.

O'Toole reported in and waited while Marty put through a few requests for replacement materials and repair work. Midford looked at the request form and scowled.

"I'll turn your ship over to Emory. He seems to be able to dig enough stuff out of the junk heap back of the shop to fix up any sort of a crate."

"Where to now?" Marty asked O'Toole.

"I ought to stick pretty close. Some more Japs might come over," O'Toole said.

"You won't be off the ground until Rivers gets his crate patched up," Midford cut in.

"In that case I guess I'll have a snack." O'Toole grinned widely. "I had to hurry my breakfast."

"I'll have a couple of glasses of cold buttermilk with you," Marty said.

In the coffee room they found several officers. The men nodded to Marty and O'Toole but went on talking. One of them said:

"I think the commander was wrong in declaring Manila an open city. The Japs are savages. They'll bomb it anyway," one captain said.

"What's that?" O'Toole demanded sharply.

The captain looked at him. "Where have you been?" he asked sharply.

"Upstairs cleaning out Uncle's attic," O'Toole answered with a grin.

"Rivers and O'Toole just got in from air action," a lieutenant explained.

"So you are the birds who just put on the big

show." The captain shot out his hand. "Shake. You certainly turned back those Jap bombers. That's what I mean. They can be held off."

Marty shook his head. "We broke it up and shot down a few but we have only one plane that can take off, left out of that mess."

O'Toole had been thinking the news over. He made his opinion short and to the point.

"The general is right. He's the rightest general in the world." He looked at the captain. "If he says it's best to make Manila an open city, I'm for it."

"If they bomb Manila now, they'll pay later," Marty said grimly.

The lieutenant nodded. "It's the long pull," he said. "Just you wait."

Everyone nodded. It was the long pull. Stabbing a man in the back gives an advantage to the assailant, but does not mean a little runt can lick a big, tough fellow.

O'Toole ordered a steak, but could not get it so switched to a double order of shoestring potatoes and a whole pie with a couple of pots of coffee on the side. Nobody else seemed hungry. Marty had his buttermilk sent in. They ate and drank in silence.

The other officers hurried away. The distant thunder of guns told them that men were fighting desperately somewhere to the north and to the south. The air was hot and close in the room. It held an ominous feeling that made Marty want to get out-of-doors.

FOR DAYS Marty and O'Toole, with the expert help of Sergeant Emory, had been working on the Grummans. O'Toole was tireless and savage in his attack upon problems which seemed impossible to solve. Marty worked silently, kept his temper and help calm the boll weevil when he began hurling wrenches because he couldn't fit a Curtiss part into his Grumman.

Much had happened since the grounding of Flight Seven for the repair of the last two planes. Manila had been bombed by a group of low flying killers. They had nosed over to make sure the requirements of an open city were carried out.

187

When they were sure no guns would blast them or pursuit ships go up they had wheeled back to unload at will.

Marty and O'Toole had watched the blasting of the helpless city from the top of a building. Ancient Santo Domingo Church had been smashed into smoking ruins; also Santo Thomas University, the Legislature and many other old landmarks which had stood for hundreds of years.

"The dirty yellow heathens," O'Toole growled. "I'm heading back to the shop. When I get my crate working I'll even up a bit for that."

So they were back at work in the shop. Now there was no black-out in the city and no protecting soldiers there. The people waited and hoped that MacArthur's weary lines would hold to the south so that the yellow horde would not plunder the capital.

But every day the news was bad. The defenders of Luzon were moving back, shortening their lines, filling the gaps because there were no reserves to send in. Marty began to worry about getting the Grummans into the air before the Japs closed in.

Their field was nothing but a flat acreage of farm land with a shop and several other buildings on it. It lay to the north of the city. Most of the buildings had been blasted. The shop had escaped air raids because it was hidden by trees.

Marty knew the general's strategy. He had played war games in the old days, and they had always carried the games through to the worst possible problems. The general was swinging around, moving back slowly and pulling his men in toward the narrow Bataan Peninsula, north and west of the city, where he would have a rugged coast on one flank, mighty Corregidor Fortress at his back, with only a rugged jungle strip to defend.

The general had no Maginot Line on which to fall back. His fighting force was faced by at least two hundred thousand Japs, while he had but thirty thousand men. His defense would be a series of strong points, machine gun nests, batteries of 75's and 155's, stretching across the peninsula's hilly, roadless top. And here he must stop his retreat and make his final stand, to the end.

Marty and O'Toole worked with a small radio blaring from a bench beside them. O'Toole was grease-smeared and his lean, hard face was lined with weariness. There had been no sleep for the two marines. They had split their few men into details and allowed them rest. But they had gone on working, hoping to get the Grummans into the air before the Japs closed in.

Two sentries had been posted on a pile of timbers from which they could see the approaches to the field. Marty wiped his hands on the legs of his flying suit and squinted at his ship.

"She's about patched up. But will she fly?"

Marty gave a nut another half turn and then poked his head out of the cockpit of his Wildcat.

"I could take this crate off right now if I had to."

His words were followed by those of an announcer on the radio. "We are going off the air. The Japanese are entering Manila. There will be no resistance. Everyone is urged to be calm."

The voice stopped abruptly and only the hum of tuner waves came from the speaker.

"Call in the men!" Marty snapped as he wiggled out on his plane.

Emory dropped a sheet of metal he had been working on. He hurried out to get the men who were resting in the shade of the trees behind the shop. The men entered and stood waiting.

"The Japs are taking over Manila," Marty said. "Lieutenant O'Toole and I will try to get our ships into the air before they get here. You boys are to make a retreat around the bay. You will join the forces of General MacArthur." Marty paused.

The men were plainly upset by his words. They had known Manila would not be defended, but the rapidity of the Jap advance took them by surprise.

"You may leave at once, if you wish. If any of you care to stay and lend a hand in getting us into the air we will appreciate it, but I am not ordering you to stay." He waited for their response.

For a moment there was silence. then the men

all spoke at once. They were staying. They had two machine guns and a number of rifles in the shop. Their corporal spoke for them.

"It's our job to get them up, sir. We aim to do that job."

"Thank you," Marty said simply. O'Toole grinned broadly at the men.

There was no more speech making. The men went to work on the Grummans at top speed. They wheeled Marty's ship out into the open and headed her into the wind. They were giving O'Toole's a final check when one of the sentries came running in from the lookout.

"About a hundred Japs headed this way!" he called. "They're circling up from the bay."

The men looked down the gentle slope. They were cut off from retreat. O'Toole tossed aside his wrench and stepped forward.

"Wind up my crate, boys. I'll blast a trail for you."

"Wind them both up," Marty added. "Get what guns you have ready and make a dash toward the bay shore. Lieutenant O'Toole and I will strafe them and try to scatter them for you."

The men grinned broadly. They rushed O'Toole's machine out on the line and wound both ships up. O'Toole's motor broke into a steady roar but Marty's refused to fire. Emory climbed up and began checking the complicated engine.

The roar of the Grumman's motor attracted the attention of the Japs moving up from the beach. They halted and looked toward the line of trees, then broke into a trot, their bayonets leveled. O'Toole climbed into his cockpit and gunned his motor to heat it quickly, clamping her down with the brakes to hold her.

"Two of you man a machine gun! Call in the sentries!" Marty snapped. Then he climbed up to help Emory check the ignition of his radial.

Two of the mechanics rushed out of the shop and planted a machine gun a few yards down the field, behind a pile of crates. Marty glanced down the slope and estimated that at least two hundred Japs were coming into the field. They were spreading out, crouching low, but coming on at a trot. The little squad at the shop wouldn't have a chance unless O'Toole got into the air.

O'Toole was bending toward his instrument panel, his eyes on his temperature gauge. The heat in the cylinder banks was building up slowly. With a shrug of his shoulders O'Toole gunned the Grumman savagely, kicked off his brakes and started down the field.

O'Toole went up the field, picking his way between bomb craters but giving the Grumman all she had. She hoiked her tail and suddenly lifted, just as she seemed about to crash into the line of trees bordering the field. Marty sucked in his breath sharply. Nobody but a cotton-duster used to tree hopping could have pulled that one.

O'Toole bored away, not trying to gain altitude, seeking only speed. Suddenly he tossed the Grumman straight up and dropped her over. His motor roared above the rifle fire of the Japs and the answering rattle of the machine gun manned by the mechanics.

"Good old boll weevil!" Marty shouted.

"Hurrah for Texas!" the men yelled.

O'Toole came blasting down on the close-packed ranks of the attackers. As he swooped upon them he opened up with his Brownings. Japs went down like wheat before a reaper. Those who escaped the hail of steel scrambled and rolled as they sought cover. The Grumman went up and over.

"Charge them, boys! Break through!" Marty shouted.

"We're winding up the Grumman," the corporal shouted. "Then we'll have a whack at them."

The demoralized Japs were assembling now that O'Toole was high in the air. They closed ranks and came on again. Not so many of them, but still a formidable force.

"Twist her tail!" Emory shouted.

The men wound the Grumman up and gave her a twist. She sputtered faintly and Emory worked to keep her alive. Slowly she shook off her laziness and began to roar. Marty climbed up and waited for the motor to heat.

O'Toole came back over, lower this time. But

the Japs had spread out and his attack was not so effective. They were deploying into a long line.

Marty signaled for the boys to stand clear. He had no time to wait for a nice adjustment of temperature. He pointed toward the Japs, then gave the boys the sign, thumbs up.

As the Grumman headed up-field Marty gunned her. She roared into full power this time, and careened away across the pitted field. Marty gave her all she had and wondered if he could duplicate O'Toole's tree-hopping stunt. The tail came up, but she was still bouncing along the ground and the trees were swaying toward him as though someone had tossed them into his face.

With a lift Marty hopped the Grumman off. Her wheels raked through the top leaves of the trees and she wobbled badly, but she went up. Once clear of the ground Marty began calling to O'Toole.

"Take position, Texas! Take position! We'll do a double when we dive."

He made a circle and saw O'Toole coming in. The two Grummans came down wing to wing, heading straight at the advancing Japs. The sight of those spitting engines of death was too much for the little yellow men. They broke and fled.

"Hold your fire, Texas!" Marty shouted. "We may need a few rounds."

As they went up Marty saw that the ground men were charging into the breach in the Jap lines. They had discarded the machine guns and were leaping down the hill with bayonets gleaming. With the Grummans coming back for another dive the Japs gave little attention to the handful of men racing between their lines. The boys, led by Emory, reached a strip of timber and disappeared.

O'Toole fairly raked the caps off the Japs who did not fall on their faces. He jigged his wings in crazy fashion and hopped hedges and trees.

Marty did not fly so recklessly but his landing gear raked over the scrambling Japs and kept them tumbling and crawling for cover. When the boys had gained the woods Marty called to his pal:

"Up to three thousand, Lieutenant O'Toole."

"Going up, Lieutenant Rivers," O'Toole drawled back.

Up the pair of war birds went, mounting into the sky. No Jap fighters came down on them, for they were sure no planes were left which the enemy could fly. Marty grinned as he looked down.

"Circle for observation," he ordered. "We'll do a bit of scouting for the general."

They flew wing to wing, circling high above Manila until they had located the main columns of Japanese troops and armoured units streaming in and around the city. Then they swung north for observation on artillery and tank formations.

"We'll have to spot a patch where we can set down behind the general's lines," Marty called. "Remember we're a pair of homeless birds."

"If we have to we'll perch on the limb of a tree. I feel lucky today," O'Toole called back. Then he began humming his coon hunting song.

As they penetrated further north they sighted divebombers in action, and located the main battle line in this manner. The general was swinging slowly into position in the rough country, fighting a savage rear guard action as he went.

O'Toole called in. "I'm heading out over the valley to have a look for their flying field." And he swung away from Marty and headed east while the latter circled the battle lines.

The divebombers were coming in low, making their attacks without fear of interceptors. Ground guns whammed away at them. One burst into flames and went crashing into the jungle. But there were twenty others to take its place.

With an eager grin Marty cuddled his flap-mike. "I'm going down to get me a divebomber, Texas."

"Hey, wait! You can't do that. I've spotted something over here," O'Toole called back.

"Look it over and then come on in," Marty called. "Remember we have to locate a landing spot behind the lines."

He nosed the Grumman over and went down.

The divebombers were having a picnic. Their little yellow pilots had no idea there was a Grumman Wildcat nearer than Pearl Harbor. Marty came in on the tail of a sleek, two-motored bandit that was dipping down lazily for a dive. His Brownings spat flame and steel. The bomber crumpled and tumbled toward the mass below.

Marty's dive carried him so low he could see U. S. soldiers waving their battered campaign hats at him. He was climbing upstairs for another dive when he looked east and saw that O'Toole had stirred up a hornet's nest of fighter craft. A half dozen Kariganes were after him and more were coming up. They had scored hits on his Grumman, Marty could see that much. He also saw a Jap plane spinning down out of the formation. But trailers of black smoke were twisting out behind the tail of the Wildcat.

The breaks had turned bad. He should have taken O'Toole down with him to attack the divebombers. They would have been able to do valuable service there before the fighters located them.

There was no telling what O'Toole had done to the Japs. He had certainly got one of them. Marty called to the Texan:

"Coming, Texas!"

"I must have collided with a star," O'Toole called back. "Lend a hand and we'll clean 'em out!"

The black streamer of smoke from O'Toole's plane had swelled to a billowing cloud before Marty could close in. A Karigane knifed in and raked the helpless ship. Marty hung on grimly and the Grumman shook under forced throttle. He had to go up to be in the ace spot. Neither of the Grummans had been in top trim when they took off.

Laying over he slashed in on the Jap who was finishing O'Toole off. The Karigane flashed into his windscreen and Marty let him have a short burst. The Jap shot upward and turned over, then dived in a helpless spin.

"O'Toole! Texas!" Marty called. "Hear me?"

He got no answer as he circled to drive off another Jap. O'Toole was going down and his ship was aflame. It wasn't like the Texan not to make some remark. O'Toole must have been hit. The boll weevil's Wildcat sloped off helplessly. Marty dived over it and around. As he came up two fighters tried to stab past him so as to get at the crippled Grumman. Marty kicked his Wildcat into a dive and opened up. He felt his controls stick and knew that his tail assembly had given away again.

Down he went in a spin, twisting around and around. Savagely he struggled to flatten out. The Grumman came out of the spin and flattened. Marty saw tree tops waving below him. He looked for the Japs and saw that they had gone back up. Craning his neck he saw O'Toole just as he crashed into a meadow close to a row of charred sheds. The Grumman bounced high, then rolled over and began to burn.

Marty nosed down toward the wreck. He hardly gave the meadow a glance as his wheels bumped the rough ground. Slapping on his brakes he freed himself from his harness and belt, then dived over the side.

O'Toole's lank form was draped over the edge of his cockpit, his head and arms hanging down limply. He had made a desperate effort to bail out. Shielding his face from the fire Marty caught hold of O'Toole and pulled. The Texan had been able to loosen his belt and so his body slid out of the burning ship. Marty gathered him up and raced away from the flaming Grumman.

As he ran he had an odd thought. He was thinking how O'Toole didn't seem to weigh anything at all. He was just a lank skeleton inside a tough hide. Those bones were held together by stringy, powerful muscles. Suddenly he was staggered and almost hurled on his face by a blast from behind. The tanks of the Grumman had blown up.

Reaching his own plane Marty tried to rip open O'Toole's flying suit to get at his wounds and stop the flow of blood. The Texan had a gash on his left cheek that was bloody but not fatal.

Loud yells from the direction of the charred sheds caused Marty to look that way. A squad of Jap riflemen were running toward him. Another squad had opened fire from a spot near the burning Grumman.

There was no time to revive his pal or to care for his wounds. A bullet smacked against the landing gear of the Wildcat and ricocheted past Marty's head. The charging infantrymen had their bayonets leveled and he did not have to guess what his fate would be if they got to him before he got away.

Gathering O'Toole up he lifted him into the plane and climbed up himself. He fixed his unconscious friend as comfortably as space and time would permit, then kicked the idling Grumman into life.

Across the rough field it bounced. Marty didn't have time to check the wind or to worry about the runway ahead. Jap bullets were peppering around the ship, pinging against wings and fuselage.

The Grumman protested against the rough treatment and her tail threatened to flop off completely. But Marty blasted it up and they staggered off the ground, zooming low over the encircling forest.

Marty didn't want altitude, he wanted to stay far below the Jap fighter planes patrolling his skies above. He roared along in a manner which suggested a tipsy seaman walking down a floating dock. Keeping the Grumman from turning over and nosing down was a job that kept him busy. He crossed the battle line and went on, seeking a base where there would be a hospital and doctors.

At last he spotted the base. There was no mistaking it. He was flying so low he saw the tents and the piles of supplies. But there seemed no spot for a landing because of the heavy timber. If he had not been flying close to the tops of the trees he would have missed the base, so well was it hidden.

There was a narrow road leading up to the tents with a great many soldiers on it. The soldiers scattered quickly as Marty settled down. The road might not be wide enough. Marty braced himself for a crash. O'Toole had not stirred and he felt an icy grip at his heart. It made him go ahead with his landing.

O'Toole had to be alive, he couldn't be washed out! There would be a surgeon at this base. The wheels of the Grumman hit the dirt road and bounced gently. She slid her wing-tips between two big tree trunks. Marty applied the brakes hard. This was no time for a fancy landing. The Grumman slowed down, but ahead a light tank had swung into the road and was clanking forward, threatening to make a head-on collision with the plane. The Grumman and the tank stopped rolling nose to nose. A cocky youngster popped up out of the tank.

"Get that crate out of the road!" he bellowed.

Marty ignored the irritated tank driver. He hoisted O'Toole up and shouted to a squad of men.

"Help me get this man to a doctor!"

The soldiers rushed in and the cocky non-com in the tank jumped down and ran forward. He beat the others to the Grumman and took

O'Toole from Marty. He turned and ran toward a big tent under a grove of spreading trees.

Marty leaped down and raced after him, stopping only long enough to ask the doughboys to shove the plane off the road and into shelter of the trees. He caught up with the non-com and the officer turned to him.

"That was you that knocked that divebomber into our lap?"

Marty nodded. His eyes were on O'Toole's face. O'Toole wasn't showing a sign of life.

"Where in blazes did you come from?" the non-com asked as he shoved into the big tent.

"I am Flight Seven, what's left of it," he answered.

The non-com looked about the big room but went on talking. "Wish there was a thousand of you fellows. We'd show those yellow rats in the divers."

"We'll show them anyway. Now let's get a doctor," Marty said grimly.

Doctors and medical corps men were busy at

operating tables and cots. The air was filled with the smell of ether and antiseptics. One of the doctors came forward.

"Put him here," he snapped, indicating an operating table. "Then get out, both of you."

The non-com laid O'Toole on the table and backed away.

"Thanks," Marty said. "I'll see you later."

"Mebby—I'm on my way up with my iron horse." The non-com grinned and made his way outside.

Marty did not leave the tent. He couldn't drag himself away. The doctor turned to him. His eyes flecked over the marine uniform and held for a second on Marty's wings. His voice was a bit softer when he spoke.

"Your pal is in bad shape. If you want him to have the best chance you better wait outside, Lieutenant."

"He's alive?" Marty had to know before he left.

"I'm not sure. And I don't have time to talk." The doctor's hands were moving swiftly as he slashed away O'Toole's jacket. "You go outside."

Marty went. He seated himself under a tree and mopped the clammy sweat off his forehead. He had brushed close to death many times in the past days and had not given it much thought. This was different. It was very much closer to him than any of the other cases.

Men were moving past the tent in squads and in columns. Three tanks rumbled by and were followed by a string of field green trucks. The eyes of every man were turned east. They were not downhearted but joked and shouted as they rushed toward the oncoming yellow hordes.

A corporal with a bandaged head came out of the hospital tent. He lighted a cigarette with a bandaged hand. Looking down at Marty he paused.

"How did you ever get here, sir?"

"It's a long story," Marty answered and grinned in spite of the numb feeling inside him. "The last leg of the trip was made in a Grumman Wildcat."

"The ship that landed a while ago?" The corporal seated himself on the grass and puffed at his cigarette.

"Yes," Marty answered. "How did you get here?"

"I stuck around a bridge to help hold back the Charlies while the trucks got through. It got pretty hot." The corporal grinned.

"But you held the bridge?"

"Shucks, yes," the corporal answered.

That made Marty grin again. "How many of you boys held that bridge?"

"Me and Slim."

"And you got smacked?" Marty wanted to ask what had happened to Slim but didn't. The corporal elaborated briefly.

"I didn't get hurt none, but they smacked Slim with a tank shell." He tossed aside his cigarette as though it had suddenly lost its good flavor. Then he scowled.

Marty nodded. He was suddenly seeing things a bit differently. This was war and this corporal was taking it in his stride. Very likely Slim was as close to this infantryman as he was to O'Toole.

"They'll never lick you fellows," he said.

"Naw," the corporal agreed. "Not with Mac calling signals. The more there is of 'em the more we'll knock over."

Marty got to his feet. "I have a friend in there," he said. "I'd like to find out about him."

The corporal nodded understandingly. "If he can be patched up, they'll fix him."

Marty went to the flap and looked in. The operating table where O'Toole had been placed was vacant. Marty looked around. He saw medical corps men carrying a stretcher to the back of the tent. The figure on the stretcher was wrapped in a blanket and the blanket was folded over his face. Marty sucked in his breath sharply.

"Come in." The doctor who had taken care of O'Toole spoke from beside a portable instrument case.

Marty stepped inside. The doctor slid a tray into place, then wiped his hands on a clean towel.

"That friend of yours is a tough one. He's awake and making a lot of noise. The blow on his head put him out for quite a time, I guess."

Marty wanted to shout. Instead he said, "Don't tell me what he wants. He's hungry."

The doctor laughed. "That is just what he's shouting for. He wants food, a thick steak with onions and a side order of kidneys and muffins." The doctor shook his head. "He's back five cots. You may speak to him. Tell him if he locates that food to let me join him."

Marty moved down the narrow aisle between the cots. He halted when he saw O'Toole's mop of red hair. O'Toole looked up at him out of the eye which was not covered by a bandage.

"Hi, Texas," Marty said.

"Boy, am I glad you came. You rustle me some grub," O'Toole croaked.

"I'm not in charge here, I'm just a transient tramp," Marty answered. "But I'll speak to the head man."

"I let them yaller babies slip up behind me," O'Toole said wearily. "I guess they got into the sun on me." He smiled his old smile. "And you came down and packed me out of the wreck."

"That's about it," Marty agreed.

"I saw you coming in just before I hit," O'Toole answered. "Thanks, Lieutenant Rivers, for the ride."

"You're welcome, Lieutenant O'Toole," Marty answered. He had not noticed the doctor beside him. The doctor was motioning him away. "You get some sleep, cotton-duster," said Marty.

O'Toole grinned wearily and closed his good eye. He muttered something Marty could not hear.

"He'll sleep now. The capsule I gave him is working," the doctor said. "I'll let you know how he gets on. That is, if you are here tomorrow."

"I guess I'm here for the duration," Marty answered. "I can fill in on a gun crew. I learned that job before I flew."

The doctor nodded. "I hear the general needs a few gunners," he said.

CHAPTER *11* GROUNDED

THE BATTLE of Bataan raged savagely along a rugged and irregular line. Tanks, infantry and the Sixteenth Cavalry fought side by side. Strangely enough, it was the Sixteenth Cavalry that covered itself with the largest measure of glory in the retreat to the peninsula.

In a mechanized war there might seem no place for the old fashioned horse. If the men of the Sixteenth ever heard of such foolishness they had not listened. It was the Sixteenth that made the delaying thrusts, the stands which allowed supplies, and guns and men to re-form in new positions. They did all this in addition to scouting activities, and their only grouch was over the loss of their horses.

At first those tough men of the Sixteenth amused Marty. He was an airman and had an idea horses were something you could still find on a few farms in the farm belt. He soon changed his ideas as he watched the Sixteenth rout Jap attacks and carry out counter-thrusts. The Sixteenth was very much in the battle while he and his war bird comrades were knocked out of the air.

Marty had reported to the colonel in charge of his section of the fight. He had suggested using the Grumman, after she had been patched up again, as a scout plane.

Emory and his little band of mechanics got through. They located Marty's landing road and came tramping in, their clothes in tatters from jungle thorns and their bodies lank from lack of food.

Marty saw them coming up the road and counted them. Only two were missing. He grinned as he saw the expressions of weariness vanish when they sighted the Grumman hiding in her tree hangar. Sergeant Emory tossed what was left of his hat into the air and ran forward. Marty stepped out to greet them.

"Welcome home, boys!" he said.

"Are we glad to get here!" Emory said. "We had to swim a river and we've crawled under vines and cut our way through jungles along with snakes and other animals." He grinned widely. In a moment his grin faded. "Is Lieutenant O'Toole about?" There was an anxious note in his voice.

"He's in the hospital tent and doing fine," Marty said.

"Will the Grumman fly?" Emory asked.

"She needs some work on her tail assembly," Marty answered.

"We'll make her fly if we have to tie that assembly together with some of that iron vine we've been fighting," Emory said. "Yes, sir, we'll make her fly."

"First you will report to the quartermaster. I will go along and we'll stop by the field kitchen

for grub. After you get new coveralls and hats we'll see what can be done with the Wildcat."
Marty grinned broadly.

When the squad returned to the ship they were in high spirits. A big meal and fresh clothing had done wonders. They were tired but eager to get at the Grumman. A number of them went in search of tools. Emory had spotted a little shop under a tree and headed that way.

Marty went out to have a look at the road again. He would need space for a take-off. He found a straight stretch of road over a hill from camp. It was long enough if everything went well, but it curved sharply at the lower end where it wound along the top of a steep canyon. Marty looked down into the jungle-matted depths of the gorge. If the Grumman failed to lift she would have a nice bed to land on.

Returning to base he found Emory down at the little shop. A blacksmith who did the horseshoeing for the Sixteenth Cavalry had a forge and an anvil set up. The smith had looked at the tail assembly and had made some suggestions. Emory was a bit dubious about putting strips of strap iron on the tail but Marty laughed.

"It may make her a bit tail-heavy, but she'll not twist out of line."

"But, sir, those braces are for patching tanks," Emory objected.

"Put them on, Sergeant," Marty ordered. "And get them on as soon as possible."

"The blacksmith will work only when he is not shoeing horses," Emory explained. "He is of the opinion, sir, that horses are of more importance than airplanes." Emory scowled. "In fact he says our playthings ought to be ditched so we could help do some real fighting."

"Off the back of a horse?" Marty asked with a smile.

"That seems to be his idea, sir," Emory said.

"He's more than half right. The Sixteenth Cavalry has done a great job. But this war will be won in the air." Marty's smile widened. "However, don't argue with him. Get what help you can, as soon as you can."

"I'll do most of the work, but I cannot weld with a coke fire," Emory answered.

Marty nodded. Emory was used to electric welding or torch work with light alloys of high strength. He just wasn't a blacksmith.

In spite of the smith's dislike for new fangled gadgets like Grumman Wildcats he did give Emory a lot of help, and even got interested in the plane.

He was a huge Missouri mule raiser who loved mules and horses and who had joined up for that reason and because he was an expert shoer. The joining had been done twenty years before. In those twenty years he had lived in the dust of a cavalry troup and had smelled and handled horses every day. Decked out in a leather apron with his bulging arms bared he looked like a picture out of an old book.

"You say she's got sixteen hundred horse power?" he said as he stood squinting at the Grumman, a sizzling length of hot iron held in his tongs.

"That's it," Emory said.

"Don't believe it," the smith grunted. But he moved closer to the Grumman and peered at her unhooded Wasp radial. "Anyway she's put together pretty, like a watch," he said. Then he laughed a deep, booming laugh. "But I reckon I could pick the hull danged gadget up by myself. Sixteen hundred horses!" He snorted and turned his attention to the tail assembly.

Marty had been listening. He moved in closer. The smith turned upon him. Noticing Marty's rank he flipped a salute.

"How are you doing, Sergeant, got her fixed up?" Marty asked.

"I could fix her up in a minute or two, sor, but yer man, here, won't let me splice in these half inch braces," the smith answered.

"They weigh forty pounds each. They're tank braces," Emory explained.

"What is your name, Sergeant?" Marty asked.

"I'm Fat Lige. Me brother was Lean Lige. I'm from Missouri." The smith straightened and observed Marty more closely.

"I'm Marty Rivers of the marines. I appreciate your helping Sergeant Emory. We can do a lot of good, locating enemy artillery and troop concentrations, once we get this ship into the air. The general is anxious to get her up there."

"Mac wants her patched up?" the Fat Lige asked.

Marty nodded. He was speaking the truth. The general was depending upon Philippine scouts, and many times they could not get through or could not get back. It took them several days to filter through the Jap lines and back again.

"Then fixed she'll be," Fat Lige said with finality. "If this ½-inch thick stuff is too heavy we'll make the braces out of ¼-inch stuff."

Emory beamed. Marty had accomplished what Emory had been trying to do by argument, and he had done it in a few minutes. Marty moved away and the two went to work.

Fat Lige's promise was not fulfilled as quickly as he had said. The tail assembly was braced rigidly after Fat Lige had put shoes on four horses. The Sixteenth came first always with him. With the tail lined up the men began patching the Grumman and rigging her so she would fly smoothly and respond quickly to her controls.

Marty was seated in the shade watching the work. The men had all but ordered him off the job. His place was in the cockpit when the Grumman was in action. The ground work was their job. Marty was checking over in his mind some of the things he meant to do, once he got into the air again. He was startled by a familiar voice.

"Hi there, Lieutenant Rivers, me compliments, sir."

Marty started and turned around. There stood O'Toole, a broad grin on his big mouth. He had strips of tape over the wound on his head, otherwise he looked hale and hearty, though leaner than ever before.

"How did you get out of that hospital tent?" Marty demanded.

"They turned me out to take care of some boys that really got hurt," O'Toole said.

"But you can't run loose. Here, sit down." Marty tried to decide whether or not O'Toole was telling the truth when he said he had been released.

"I'm in flyin' trim," O'Toole stated. "The rap on the head knocked me out. A chunk of shell case scratched my ribs. I got a black eye and a splinter of steel still in me side. Otherwise I'm fit."

"Just the same I do the flying until the doc tells me you can go up," Marty said.

O'Toole looked eagerly at the Grumman. "Is she in trim to go up?"

"I think so," Marty answered. "I'm reporting for scouting duty tomorrow. Emory has had her turning up and she sounds swell. It's lucky they have a number of tanks powered by airplane engines, that gives us oil and gas we can use."

"You don't aim to hog all the scouting?" O'Toole asked in a grieved voice.

"No, but I aim to talk with your doctor before you go up."

O'Toole grinned. "I got him fixed. I never let up on that saw-bones for a minute. He was so glad to see me go he let me have the steak they had saved for the head man of the outfit. Fact is, he'd okayed me for flight duty right now. He'd be hopin' I'd fly a long way from here once I took off."

Marty laughed. "I'll get the truth out of him," he said grimly. "For the present you're grounded."

"I'll jest go along when you talk with him," O'Toole said.

Their voices were swallowed by the roar of the Grumman's motor. It lifted and blasted through the hot, damp jungle which crouched all around them. Well away from its slicing prop stood Fat Lige, his huge hands on his hips. His mouth was wide open in amazement. When Emory switched off the motor he bellowed.

"Man, has she got her a whinny!"

"She has power, too," Emory said proudly.

"I have her tuned up as fine as the day she came out of the factory. That's a radial for you, dependable, with as many lives as a cat."

Fat Lige shook his head as he backed away. "She reminds me o' a Clidesdale stallion me pappy once owned. Snortin' and roarin' that way."

"Roll her over the hill and hide her in the jungle," Marty ordered. "I'm reporting for duty."

O'Toole went with Marty to headquarters where they were challenged by a guard.

"Lieutenants O'Toole and Rivers reporting for service," Marty said.

The orderly spoke over his shoulder and stepped aside. Marty and O'Toole entered the tent and stood before a folding table. Four men sat behind the table, two colonels, a major and a captain. The colonel nearest them looked up and nodded.

"We have the ship ready for the air, sir," Marty said.

"Good work, Lieutenant. Pull up stools,

gentlemen, and go over this field map with me."
He ran a long finger half way down the map.
"What we wish to know is the location of artillery concentrations. We know we have gun su-
periority, and if we can locate their big guns we
can knock them out before they do any damage."

Marty and O'Toole went over the maps with
the colonel. An hour later they left and headed
back to their tent. Marty had a set of field maps
on which to mark locations.

"Flying over the lines will be a tough assignment," O'Toole said. "That is, after the Japs
discover the general has one plane left."

"It will be a game of tag," Marty agreed.

"Going right up?" There was a wistful note
in the Texan's voice.

"I'm on my way," Marty said as he got to his
feet. "You stretch out and get some rest."

"Reckon I will, after I see you take off."
O'Toole was on his feet.

They found the ground crew gathered around
the Grumman. Some of the men were dubious
about the take-off. The road was short and there

was the canyon at the end of it. But none of them doubted Marty would try it. He smiled at them as he ordered Emory to warm up the motor.

The Grumman sat in the shade, her prop blast making the jungle vines dance and weave. The boys rolled her out and Marty got in and revved her up against the brakes. She was hitting smoothly and her engine temperature was right. Heating her up with the air around her at one hundred was no big job. Marty gave her the gun but held her in place.

With his indicator needle rolling far over he turned her loose, and with a lift of his hand he was off. The Grumman blasted her tail up at once and roared down the road. Marty gave her all she had, but let her ride the road the whole way. As the canyon leaped toward him and the shrubbery on its edge reached out to tangle the wheels of the Wildcat he jumped her off. She surged upward and Marty saw the men on the ground waving.

He circled the base and headed for the firing

line where the big guns were blasting away. Smoke was rolling up from a low ridge. He knifed over the tree tops, his speed building up to nearly three hundred miles per hour. For the first time in many days the Grumman responded quickly to his touch. The tail assembly seemed solid and strong. But the motor was a little slower. Marty figured she would not be so snappy in a fight.

He swept over the line of fire and spiralled upward, laying over to look down. So far, he had drawn no fire at all. He sighted lines of Jap troops marching along narrow roads. In a clump of trees he spotted a battery and jotted down its position.

The Japs had made no effort at all to camouflage their artillery positions. They were sure no enemy planes were left in the air, so were not worried about prying eyes. So Marty was able to chalk down the positions of a dozen batteries.

As he ducked along over the enemy lines Marty called the locations back to the men in the radio control room. The men at Operations headquarters marked down the locations on their maps.

"Can you stand by to check fire for us on point three—crossroads and creek, with red bridge on left? We are about to open fire? Do you hear me, Rivers?"

"You are coming in loud and clear, Operations. Rivers standing by."

Marty swung around and headed back toward the crossroads and the red bridge where he had reported heavy concentrations of field guns. As he went back he drew some gunfire, but it was weak and the shots very wild.

"If we only had a squadron of bombers," Marty muttered. "These Charlies are wide open." The temptation to swoop down and rake them was strong. A tank column was moving up a narrow road. They were rolling along in close formation, three abreast and in a long line. "What a target!" Marty growled. He called in the location of the tanks. The boys with the seventy fives and the one fifty fives would give that tank group a surprising welcome.

As he went over the red bridge he saw that the Japs were swarming around their guns, ready to go into action. He idled down and slid along with machine gun bullets zipping around him. Smoke was puffing up from the jungle ridge where the general had a battery concealed. The guns clustered near the bridge were suddenly enveloped in great clouds of dust. Chunks of metal and wood sailed high above the spurting explosions. Jap gunners were running out of the dust and the smoke, plunging into the woods. The general's gunners were very accurate. Great blossoms of fire and dust spread slowly, eating up the Jap gun positions.

"Rivers calling! Rivers calling! Do you hear me?"

"We hear you loud and clear, Rivers. Come in."

"A hundred yards north. Guns in woods a hundred yards north. You are moving fire too far south," Marty called.

Going on over he came back. The gun cluster to the north was a smoking pile of twisted metal.

From somewhere below an anti-aircraft gun opened up—the first Marty had encountered. Then a shell burst under the Grumman, hurling her fifty feet into the air. She came out of the sudden up-surge with her motor hammering away, but Marty could feel cold air funneling in around his feet.

With only one plane to concentrate on, the archie was laying them in very close. Marty opened the throttle and roared away. Other guns joined in and he decided to go up out of range—but not too high for there would be plenty of Japs upstairs. But he also wanted to get a wider view of the operations so he began to go up. He was boring along above the muck when he sighted four Jap interceptors coming down the chute at a roaring pace, eager to knock down the Grumman. Marty wanted badly to swing up and have a whack at them, but he had his orders. No dogfights.

Ducking, Marty went down through the barrage of bursting shells. With steel flying all around him he twisted and dived and ducked.

It wasn't much safer down close to the ground, now that the Japs had opened up on him. But the Kariganes did not come on down.

He was twisting and rolling to reduce the chances of a hit when he sighted a mass of Jap infantry moving up a slope. They had driven a wedge into the American lines and were threatening to flank a battery of big guns. He saw that a thin line of cavalry was in action, but that they were giving ground before the massed attack.

Laying over Marty went down. He nosed into the massed infantry. With the green mat of jungle rushing up to meet him he squeezed his gun button. The surprise of the attack, combined with the deadly fire of the eight Brownings, caused wild confusion.

The Japs ducked and rolled and fled. As Marty went up he saw the thin line of cavalry charging. The Sixteenth was taking advantage of the support he had given them. Behind the cavalry came men with bayonets. Marty circled back and watched the rout.

"Rivers! Rivers! Operations calling. Do you hear me?"

"I hear you, Operations. Rivers on patrol."

"Return to base, Rivers. Report to your H.Q."

"Coming in," Marty called back.

He zoomed up and sailed back over his own lines. Dropping in low over the canyon he hit the road and skidded to a stop, close to the tree hangar that the men had chopped out of the jungle.

The ground men ran forward and tucked the Grumman away as soon as Marty climbed down. He gave a few instructions and hurried away toward the headquarters tent.

CHAPTER *12* GUNNERS

MARTY LOOKED in on O'Toole before reporting to the colonel. He was sleeping soundly, his mouth open and his snores rumbling softly. Marty dropped the tent flap and hurried away.

At Colonel Miller's tent there was great activity. The space inside the tent was hot, and the air close and thick with cigar smoke. Men worked at tables and on ammunition cases—anywhere they could find space. The colonel looked up from a portable table that swayed on its thin, folding legs.

"Come in, Lieutenant Rivers. Pull up a

stool." The colonel mopped his brow with a large handkerchief and leaned back.

Marty set a stool beside the table and sat down. The colonel leaned forward and pulled a map from a pile on his desk.

"You did excellent work today, Lieutenant. Colonel Denby of the Sixteenth Cavalry sent over a word of thanks for support at Hill Seven." The colonel smiled. "When Denby admits he needed support and got it from anything but a horse, that is high praise. We need more planes, but we won't get them, unless the boys over near the coast can patch up a few of the P–40's we dragged down there."

"You had a job for me?" Marty asked.

"A scout just came through enemy lines to tell us of an oil and ammunition dump in the valley. It seems the enemy is so sure of his mastery of that territory that the oil and the explosives have been stored together. There are four big tanks." The colonel smiled broadly.

"What we need is a couple of Curtiss Helldivers," Marty said.

"We do not have bombers, but Sergeant Emory from your crew, is a very resourceful boy. He has designed a bomb we can make and one you could drop on that dump. Once you set fire to the oil tanks the ammunition will go up. If you touch off the ammunition the oil will burn." The colonel chuckled.

"What sort of bomb has Emory designed?" Marty asked cautiously.

"I'll call the sergeant in. He's working in the next tent." The colonel motioned to an orderly and when the man stepped forward he said:

"Have Sergeant Emory report to me at once."

It was clear Emory had sold the colonel on his idea. Marty wondered what sort of gadget it was. So far in this war he had flown more queer ships and handled more crazy assignments than a flier making a county fair circuit with a flying circus.

Sergeant Emory came in with a sheet of paper. He saluted and stood waiting. "Pull up a stool, Sergeant, and let me have your drawing."

The colonel flattened the paper before Marty. Marty looked at Emory.

"Suppose you explain it briefly, Sergeant," he said.

Emory flushed and bent over his design. "I have fixed up a hundred pounds of dynamite and added some incendiary materials. This charge is attached to a percussion cap and fuse. The release mechanism is being built by Fat Lige, I mean Sergeant Lige, sir."

"You mean I light a fuse before releasing this bomb?" Marty asked doubtfully.

"Yes, sir. We have rigged a lighter that will work in a high wind. It is really a lighter Sergeant Lige got for Christmas several years ago —from his wife."

Marty laughed softly and bent over the design. "I hope Fat Lige has done a good job on the release. I'd hate to be flying around with a hundred pounds of dynamite attached to a lighted fuse, and not be able to shake it loose."

"I am sure the principle is sound," Emory said.

"But will it work?" Marty insisted.

"It works," Emory assured him.

"I am satisfied." Marty shoved the drawing

aside and faced the colonel. "Give me the exact location of my objective, sir."

The colonel was not smiling when he answered. "We appreciate your undertaking this, Rivers. I will make a personal citation."

"Thank you, sir," Marty said. He was on his feet. "I'll be off."

Emory went with him and they hurried down to the shop of Fat Lige. He had gone up to where the Grumman was parked so they followed.

A few minutes later Marty was inspecting the bomb which the men had already attached to the undercarriage of the Grumman. The release device looked practical. Fat Lige was very much excited over the whole scheme.

"She's a winner by at least five lengths," he crowed. "Unless some Jap pots her with a bullet before you get rid of her."

"She is, if the Wildcat can get off the ground in the short run we have. If not, we ought to clear most of the trees out of the bottom of that canyon," Marty said.

Emory passed over the lighter. It was a huge affair made of brass in the shape of a cylinder. A long chain hung from one end. The idea was that the open end of the cylinder shielded the flame for wind, making the lighter a pot of fire similar to a blow torch. Marty grinned broadly as he turned the lighter over.

"Me old lady sent it so's I could light me pipe whilst ridin' a hoss at full speed in a Kansas cyclone," Fat Lige explained.

"I twist this wheel and then shove the pot of fire down over the fuse?" Marty asked.

"You spin that wheel and the flint lights the wick. Then you shove the lighter down over the end of the fuse. We have pulled the fuse up through a bullet hole in the bottom of the ship and taped it lightly into place. When the fuse starts spitting you have time for about half a minute of sighting. The load should be dropped from about fifteen hundred feet altitude to have it explode after it hits and not in the air," Emory explained. "But it will go off even if it lands and lies for a few seconds."

"It will also go off if I don't get rid of it?"

"It would, sir," Emory agreed.

"It's a swell job. Just you fellows climb a tree and put your field glasses on the valley." Marty grinned.

"I allers had a hankerin' to take a ride in one of them flyin' machines, but I wouldn't go up with you today unless you was headed for To-kio," Fat Lige said.

"Get her warmed up," Marty ordered. "I want the engine tuned up and plenty hot before I take off." Marty was studying his maps. He had to go up over the muck to avoid a chance hit. That meant he had to fly through patrolled air.

Emory gave orders and the men wheeled the Grumman out and began tuning her up. The roaring of the motor wakened O'Toole and he came out of his tent, blinking and yawning. He said nothing until he had walked clear around the Grumman.

"You get some funny ideas," he said at last. "Slick?"

"Looks like you'd be on foot along with me, after this trip. Where you headed for? Goin' to blow Tokio off the map?" O'Toole squinted at the odd looking bomb.

"I'm paying a brief call over the lines," Marty explained.

"She won't fly anyway but straight ahead or straight down with that cargo," O'Toole said.

"I have only a short run before cutting loose," Marty explained. "Just out over the valley."

"You ought to let me take her. I got Lady Luck in me pocket all of the time," O'Toole said eagerly.

"No," Marty answered. "Doc says no flying for you until he gives the O.K."

O'Toole glowered darkly, "I'd better stayed in that hospital tent. They treated me better there."

Emory came up and saluted. "She's ready, sir."

Marty grinned at the Texan. "Keep a light in the window for me," he said. "I'll be right back."

He climbed into the Grumman, adjusted his goggles and had a last inspection of the mechanism for releasing and for lighting the bomb. With a lift of his fist, thumb up, he opened the Wasp wide and held her with his brakes. She roared and strained, but Marty clamped her down until his motor was turning up at maximum. Then he kicked her loose.

She bored down the narrow road, gaining speed with every yard. The edge of the canyon loomed under the nose and Marty bounced her off. He held his breath as the air smacked him and sent the Grumman upward. The bomb did not yank loose. Marty settled back against his shock pad. Slowly the ship lifted as he circled inland away from the Jap lines. He had to build altitude for a slope toward his target.

As he banked and headed for his objective he noticed that the Japs had not been asleep. His sweep over the battle had put them on the alert. They had also thought about the vulnerable supply dump. A flock of fighter planes cut back and forth over the target.

This called for a change in tactics. He had to come in fast and dive on his target to make sure he did not miss. And he had to get in with as little maneuvering as possible. After he was rid of his bomb he could fight it out with the enemy. But with a ship that was trimmed for straight flight he could not fight until he was free of his cargo.

Going back and up he checked the valley below. He could see the oil tanks and the dump of shells. Nosing over he went down the chute at a roaring pace. The Kariganes spotted him as he came in, but he did not change his course. Any Jap that got in front of him would get a dose from his Brownings. Those settling on his tail would have a fast ride.

Then he saw that the Japs had moved a circle of anti-aircraft guns in around the dump. The archies had set up a terrific fire that filled the sky over the dump with steel. Marty grinned. In the center of that ring of muck there had to be an opening. The Japs couldn't risk having their own steel dropping on the ammunition and the oil tanks. He'd have to come almost straight down to hit the hole in that fiery doughnut, but he could do that, too.

The Kariganes closed in from every angle as the Grumman dived toward its target. Three came in from the left and four from the right. Three more knifed up in a head-on rush. Marty held his course and thumbed his gun button. He meant to slope in above the ground fire and then dive into the circle inside the barrage.

As the three up-surging Japs came into range Marty pressed his gun button. He rolled his ship a bit to give his lead the effect of a saw. The Japs were dropping lead at him at the same time, but their gun power was less than that of the Grumman.

In a flash there was only one Karigane coming up at him. Two had vanished from sight. The lone pilot came on, but Marty could see he was wavering as bullets ripped at his wings and fuse-lage. With a desperate twist he went over and off to the right.

Marty now saw the ring of clear air inside the

circle of bursting shells. He set the Grumman on her tail and nosed down, cutting his motor to brake his vertical dive. The maneuver shook three Japs off his tail and freed him from a hail of lead, pounding in from his right. He flipped the wheel on the lighter. An orange flame blossomed inside the cylinder. He waited to see that it would stay lit. The flame increased.

Looking down through his windscreen he checked his target and glanced at his altimeter —ten thousand feet. He shoved the lighter down over the fuse sticking up through the floor plates. For a second nothing happened, then sparks began to shoot out around the white cord of the fuse. Marty flipped the top on the lighter, extinguishing its flame. He set his sight on a big tank close to a shell dump.

The Grumman was plummeting to earth at a terrific pace. Marty checked his altitude—four thousand feet. He held on, worrying now over whether he had lighted the fuse at the right time. His hand slid over to the release lever. The dump below was rising to meet him. His eyes flecked to his instrument panel—two thousand feet. Sweat was breaking out on his forehead and trickling down along his nose and inside his goggles.

Slowly he pulled up on the lever. The Grumman kept on roaring down. Marty jerked hard. He had to cut loose soon or go down with his bomb. Then he noticed that the fuse had disappeared and a curl of smoke was coming in through the bullet hole where it had been.

It looked just as though he would smack the biggest oil tank. Suddenly the Grumman jerked and lifted. Marty pulled her up hard and felt a momentary blackness sweep in on him. He shook his head and strained against the controls. His brain cleared with a snap. He was going up at a terrific rate, going up and about to go over in a loop. Easing off he dropped away on one wing, just to make sure he wasn't raked as he leveled off.

As he laid over he saw that a Karigane had gone down on his tail. The Jap had not been able to pull out of his dive. Marty never knew whether it was the exploding Karigane or his bomb that set off the dump. The whole earth seemed to be rising up in a great mushroom of debris and smoke. A moment later pillars of flame and black smoke leaped high above the dump.

Something heavy hit his right wing with terrific impact, ripping a ragged hole in it. Another chunk of steel blasted in and smashed through his instrument board. The ground guns had found him.

The Grumman struggled on up above the gunfire. As she began to reach the top of her steep climb her radial coughed uncertainly. It coughed again, sputtered twice, then went dead. Where his ears had been filled with the roar of power now Marty was blanketed with silence, broken only by the scream of the wind through the exposed ribs of his wing.

With a heave he nosed over and dived in a long slope toward the general's lines. He had a quick glimpse of three fighters roaring down upon him. He saw no more because a sheet of flame hit him in the face. It came glancing back from the cowling of his motor. Pawing and choking Marty freed his belt and crawled to the edge of the cockpit.

Dragging himself free of his seat he rolled out and went down. The first thing he did was to fill his lungs with fresh air. Then he just fell, pawing himself into an upright position.

His job now was to hold on and not open his chute until he was close to the ground. The Japs were circling and diving, waiting for his silk to blossom out so that they could riddle him as he hung helpless in the air.

He was coming down fast, faster than he liked falling. The tree tops began reaching for his boots. Marty pulled the rip cord and felt the pilot chute give a gentle tug. Then his silk bellied out and he got a sharper jerk. A moment later he was settling down very slowly.

The Kariganes came down and potted at him, but they had no desire to mow down jungle trees. Marty selected a small clearing and began working the ropes in an effort to reach it.

He was back of the enemy lines and did not want to be hung up on a tree for Jap infantry target practice.

His efforts guided him into a clearing choked with underbrush and vines. His chute billowed out and folded up. The landing was perfect except for the mass of jungle growth he had settled into. Hurriedly he began freeing himself from his harness. As he slipped free the last snap he heard a rifle crack, then another. A machine gun rattled. Bullets screamed over his head. Marty dived down into the green tangle.

He could hear men shouting and knew they were slashing their way toward him. He began to crawl, squeezing between giant creepers and pulling aside rank mosses. He had no knife to clear a pathway so the going was slow. Thorns ripped his clothing and knife-sharp grasses cut his hands and face. Finally he halted and sat listening.

There seemed to be Japs all round his hiding place. Guns were popping, and on his right he heard the rumbling roar of artillery. He turned away from the blasting and listened. Off on his left artillery was answering. That would be the Americans. He got down on his hands and knees and began worming his way forward.

After working out of the choked clearing Marty was able to stand up and look around. The growth had thinned out except for heavy timber which grew so densely that it made the world below its leafy canopy a place of shadows and twilight. Marty made sure of the direction of the American guns and headed in that direction.

The going got rougher and he found himself on a steep slope. So far he had not met any Japs but he wasn't taking any chances. Marty moved slowly and stopped to listen every few yards. Even with all this care he suddenly stumbled into the midst of a company of infantry. And before he was aware of it he was in the middle of a charge up the hill.

The jungle had been still except for the distant booming of big guns. Marty was peering out at an open hillside when suddenly the whole slope seemed to explode. Machine guns began hammering and larger pieces blasted. From the ground, it seemed, there came a great swarm of Japanese armed with rifles. They charged up the hill and as they ran many of them tossed firecrackers ahead of them. The noise was terrific, and Marty craned his neck to see what the enemy's objective could be.

As far as he could tell there wasn't anything on the slope above. Certainly there was no answering fire. The Japs swept up the slope in a mass, which literally trampled down the jungle growth. Below the infantry tanks were coming up, dragging field guns. Little yellow men went by in squads, packing heavy machine guns.

Marty ducked deeper into the embrace of a great creeper and watched. He even climbed ten feet from the ground for a better look. And as he wiggled around to see up the slope, things began to happen high on the hill.

The general's artillery opened up. Marty clutched the creeper and wrapped his arms around the trunk of the tree which supported the vine. The ground shook and the tree wavered and swayed, almost tossing Marty out of his ambush. A shell had landed close to the edge of the jungle. When the dirt and leaves settled there was a big crater. The squad of twenty Japs who had been in that spot a moment before had vanished.

It seemed the whole open slope was exploding. The even, deep-packed ranks of the Jap infantry had become a churned and scrambling mass of yellow men scrambling for cover. Marty saw that most of those on his side of the clearing were heading for the jungle.

Sliding down out of the tree Marty made a charge of his own—up the hill. His only pause was long enough to ambush a Jap who plunged into the timber, almost bumping into him. A right hook to the jaw put the Jap to sleep. Marty caught up his rifle and ammunition belt.

After the first terrific smash of the American artillery the Japs re-formed in the woods and in the shell holes on the slope. Marty saw that they were going on up and that there were still hundreds of them.

He raced on, panting and sweating, keeping ahead of the Japs who were taking cover. The fact that the enemy had avoided the dense woods in their charge saved him from being in the midst of their forces.

His first halt came when a bullet from above screamed through the bushes where he was thrashing and flailing about in an effort to break through. Marty crouched down and worked his way carefully forward. He stuck his helmet and goggles on the Jap bayonet and held it high. A voice called to him:

"Stick up yer head and let me have a look!"

Marty stood up and stepped out.

"Come on up, leatherneck!" the voice shouted.

Marty dashed up the hill and rolled into a fox hole in the bank just as a hail of bullets raked the slope. An infantryman sat in the hole. He was working a Springfield with deliberate care.

"Where'd you come from?" he asked out of the side of his mouth.

"Shot down behind the lines," Marty answered. He had rolled over and was working the light Jap rifle.

"We saw you touch that dump off. Only trouble is they still got too much ammunition." The rifleman paused, then his Springfield roared. "This is their fifth charge. If we can keep the big babies pounding 'em we'll hold. But last time they got right up to the guns and this time they may take 'em over."

"Where are the batteries?" Marty asked.

"Back a little ways. They got us shoved right back under the big fellows. I've never seen so many Japs in all my life. Its like a grasshopper plague. You can't knock enough of them off to slow 'em up."

"I'm a gunner," Marty said. "I'll go back and lend a hand."

"Good, cause I'm going to have to go down after them Charlies with the steel." The infantryman began worming his way out of the fox hole.

Marty climbed out and worked his way back. He was challenged a number of times and each time he asked the location of the batteries. He came upon the first pair of 145's in a clump of trees. The crew of the gun nearest him was shorthanded. A man with a bloody bandage on his head was serving the breech. His powder-blackened face was drawn and taut and he staggered as he strained at the shell rack. Marty leaped forward and caught the gunner as he swayed and pitched forward.

He laid the gunner back in the shade and leaped to the breech. Smoke swirled around them as a light wind swept it back from the muzzles of their guns. The noise was so terrific there was no use in trying to say anything. If the rest of the crew noticed the change they did not slow down in their frantic efforts to keep the big gun hammering away.

Marty sweated and worked. He had no time to strip down and his flying suit was clinging to him like a rag when the big gun suddenly ceased firing. All along the line the guns went silent. Somebody laughed. The man next to Marty shouted.

"They routed 'em. Hurray for the infantry!"

Marty turned quickly to face the speaker. He

stared at the powder-blackened face, then he laughed as loud as any of the men.

"Texas, you cotton-dusting old buzzard!"

"How are you, Lieutenant Rivers?" O'Toole asked as he wiped a streak of black out of his eyes.

"We wind up in the same crew," Marty said.

"It's a good job," O'Toole said. "Plenty of excitement."

"It will do until we can get some wings under us again," Marty agreed.

"I figure we'll be on this here betsy quite a spell," O'Toole answered.

"We'll be right here when the marines take over again down at Manila," Marty answered.